DALRIADA
A Romance

Christopher Harvie, born Motherwell, 1944, educated St Boswells, Kelso, Edinburgh Royal High School and Edinburgh University. Lecturer, Open University, 1969–80, Professor, Tuebingen University since 1980. Married to the late Virginia Roundell until her death in 2005, father of Alison. Harvie has been writing history and broadcast scripts since 1962; last count, sixteen books; three in their fourth editions. *Dalriada* is his first fiction. Harvie has been teacher, commentator, politician and contrarian, in Scotland, Britain and Germany, guest-lecturing from Perm in the Urals to Laramie in the Rockies. He now shares part of a Victorian house outside Melrose (from September 2015 joined to the modern world by train) with his bicycle, near-centenarian father and the spirit of Walter Scott.

As to *Dalriada*, he treasures George Roy Hill's epigraph to Laramie's most famous movie, *Butch Cassidy and the Sundance Kid* – 'Most of the facts in this film are true.'

Capercaillie Books

DALRIADA
A Romance of Invention

Christopher Harvie

Capercaillie Books

First published by Capercaillie Books Limited in 2015.

Registered Office Summit House, 4-5 Mitchell Street, Edinburgh EH6 7BD.

© Christopher Harvie

A catalogue record of this book is available from the British Library

ISBN 978-1-909305-88-5

Printed by Bell and Bain Ltd, Glasgow

In memory of Arthur Marwick, 1936–2006
historian and teacher

Contents and Cast List

(Note: * based on real people, the others are fictional)

Chapter 1: The Rainbow Bridge · pages 13–40

Alexander Birnbaum (1890–1970)	German civil servant, later American economist
Bob Cormack MP (1892–1956)	trade union leader, foreman at Ballantyne Muir shipyard, musician
Matthias Duerr (1887–1973)	Swiss soldier and artist, later industrialist
Adam Halley (1876–1957)	later Andrew Henderson iron broker, musician, spy
Quentin Kennedy, Lord Westermain MP (1890–1919?)	adventurer
*David Herbert Lawrence (1882–1930)	novelist, poet and artist
Helena Mann (1890–1919)	secret agent and socialist organiser
*Dr Osborne Henry Mavor, 'James Bridie' (1888–1951)	physician and dramatist
Dr, later Sir Duncan Muir MP (1886–1966)	shipbuilder and shipowner
Constance Reid (1889–1942)	Lady Chatterley, later Mrs Parkin and Frau Goesler
Catherine Reid (1892–1986)	partner and later wife of Sir Duncan Muir
*Frieda von Richthofen, later Lawrence (1879–1956)	his wife
Ernest Robertson (1894-1965)	inventor
Myra Gemmill Wark (1896–1990)	dancer
Lady Emily Watson-Gordon (1885–1915)	wife to Duncan Muir
Watson Wilson (1894–1935) 'Mr Memory'	cook and music-hall artist

Baron Winfried von und zu Stumm (1890–1939) — German diplomat

Chapter 2: 'Blow Bugle Blow!' · pages 41–69

*Colonel John Buchan (1875–1940) — writer and intelligence agent, later MP and as Lord Tweedsmuir Governor-General of Canada

*Richard Burdon, Viscount Haldane (1856–1928) — Lord Chancellor of England

*David Lloyd George MP (1859–1945) — Liberal, May 1915 Minister of Munitions, late 1916 Prime Minister

Walter Innes (1830–1919) — Scots-American steel magnate

Lucas Kelly (1884–1957) — later O'Brien, trade unionist and Communist

Captain Angus MacGillveray (1875–1954) — of MI5

*Charles Masterman (1874–1927) — Liberal politician and propagandist

Sir David Paterson, WS, MP (1892–1965) — Scottish politician, later lawyer

*King George V, 1865–1936

*Frances Stevenson, later Countess Lloyd George (1888–1972)

*William Weir, Viscount Weir (1877–1959) — Clyde Munitions Controller, later Air Minister

Chapter 3: Daedelus · pages 70–111

Major Hubert de Bridoon (1876–1917) — cavalryman, later aviator

Dr Larry Doyle (1874–1955) — engineer

John Reede (1893–1973) — American journalist and Democrat senator

*Sir Daniel Stevenson (1851–1944)	Lord Provost of Glasgow, coal merchant, peace campaigner, philanthropist
*Andrew Bonar Law MP (1858–1923)	Conservative businessman and party leader
*John Wheatley MP (1880–1930)	Labour councillor, Health Minister
*James Maxton MP (1885–1946)	Labour agitator and organiser
*George Bernard Shaw (1855–1950)	dramatist and political writer
*Wilhelm Groener (1867–1939)	German general, later war minister
Kuno Liebeskind (1875–1919)	German radical
Avril Halley, later Lady Rattray and Viscountess Mountbullock (1886–1969)	philanthropist

Chapter 4: 'A Poor and Sinful Creature' · pages 112–147

*William Maxwell Aitken, Hector Henry Astor (1879–1952)	American financier
*Lord Beaverbrook (1879–1964)	press baron
Sir John Kierlaw, Bart, (1835–1930)	cotton-master
Monsignor Emilio Carracci (1862–1937)	Papal Nuncio in the United Kingdom
Frederick, Count Gondremark (1840–1925)	former Chief Minister of Gruenewald
*Father John Gray (1866–1934)	aesthete, poet and essayist
*Timothy Michael Healy (1855–1931)	Irish politician
Charles Foster Kane (1880–1937)	American press magnate
*Montagu Compton Mackenzie (1883–1972)	writer and Scots nationalist
*Somerset Maugham (1874–1965)	novelist and spy
Monsignor Federigo Pallanzi (1875–1955)	Vatican diplomat
*Pope Benedict XV (1854–1922)	Giacomo della Chiesa
Father Roger Rothschild SJ (1875–1960)	

Chapter 5: Eastern Approaches · pages 148–182

*William Earsman (1884–1965)	Communist, later Labour Councillor
*Peter Petrov (floreat 1910–20)	Communist and Russian agent
*Joseph Roth (1894–1939)	Austrian novelist
Sonya Serebriakova, later Cormack (1890–1944)	cook
Ivan Yevgrav, engineer (1898–1942)	Russian soldier and aviator

Chapter 6: Resurrections · pages 183–197

*Sir James Matthew Barrie (1860–1937)	dramatist
*Commandant Michael Collins, (1890–1922)	guerrilla, TD and Minister
*Joseph Conrad (1857–1924)	sailor and novelist
*Tom Johnston MP (1881–1965)	Scottish Labour leader
Jeeves, (Pelham Grenville?) (1881–1975)	valet to the above
*Neil Munro (1863–1930)	editor and novelist

Locations

The action plays in west coast Scotland, London, Berlin, *Mitteleuropa*, and Russia, east coast America and Canada between 1912 and 1939.

LANDKARTE CLYDE~MÜNDUNG, 1912: HELENA MANN, ZEICHN~ERIN

1

The Rainbow Bridge

On second cities, and the chamber music of total war.

Aimez-vous Brahms?

> *Come to the window*
> *It is beastly derk!*
> *The warlocks are dencing*
> *In the West End Perk!*
> *Come to the window,*
> *Thy lover brave to see.*
> *For only I am here,*
> *And there's nobody here but me!*

Dr Osborne Mavor pirouetted, flourished his hands. Light from the electrolier gleamed on his Pickwick pince-nez,

'Applause! Applause!'

Far below the Muir flat in lofty Park Terrace the yellow-lighted cage of a tram sparked and whined its way west into the gloaming. The small invited audience perched on an assortment of parlour chairs, the quartet before the great window, Dr Muir facing his baby grand. Dr Mavor introduced:

'Fraulein Mann, student of English and the dismal science.'

Helena smiled, bowed slightly in her working pinafore frock, shifted her viola to her chin.

'Mr Adam Halley, of the Iron Ring.' The still-youngish face atop the big black moustache was impassive, behind the cello's scroll.

'Comrade Bob of the *Vorwaerts*, the Niel Gow *de nos jours*. Such learning!' Engineer Cormack struck with his fiddle a soulful Raeburn pose.

The host, always slightly tense, nodded, pulled up his piano stool, adjusted his eyeglasses. Mavor, he reflected, has had just enough to make him eloquent and thank God no more.

'Friends! At last! The Opus 25 piano quartet. Brahms's unknown symphony!'

'The Glasgow Symphony?' They knew their Vaughan Williams.

Among the invitees a small serious-faced man stood and bowed: Brahms' own pianist Frederic Lamond, his friend in the last Viennese years. The other guests were caught up in the 'progressive' enthusiasms and music-making of Glasgow at its zenith, and to that room Helena Mann had shepherded them.

Lady Emily Muir was due back from a Suffragette conference. Housekeeper Agnes had her night off, spent with her married sister in Dalmuir. Duncan had months before run the parts off on the Ballantyne Muir shipyard's Drawing Office copier, downriver at Dumbarton.

It wasn't easy. The piano part was huge and muscular and – as Schoenberg later found – unbalanced the rest. Things were moderated by Muir's tentativeness balanced with Helena's charm and gentle coercion, in making the effort cohere. Not to speak of that setting: the window giving out on to Kelvingrove, its exhibition buildings, the new university, and below them the busy, kinetic world of trams, cranes, chimneys, masts, funnels, people and smoke.

The Opus 25 was young man's music, from 1861, seemingly boundless in ideas and invention – Schoenberg called it 'Brahms' Fifth' – ending in a pounding Hungarian gipsy-dervish dance. There was the cast of melancholy: Schumann's madness and death, unwinnable Clara's battle to recover and survive; apprenticeship in the midget court of Lippe-Detmold; the heritage of *Kapellmeister* J S Bach.

The first movement began with Bach's laconic, ugly phrase – *karg* was the German word – that compressed, chorale-like, all the 'notions' of progress, brotherhood, memory, stoicism, resumed *in extenso* in the First Symphony. They all knew *that* by heart. At the end of this sixth evening, with the street gasmantles now fully on, they had it nearly pat.

This was the public event. Coherent and increasingly confident, steady and fluent, the players responding through a quiet reliance on each others' gaze and approbation. The sense of what the Germans call *Einklang*, not just harmony but some sort of spiritual empathy – *going together*. Then, when the Hungarians had danced themselves senseless to some mighty applause, they gathered in the window and took their first proper drinks in hours.

The men turned to Helena, shy in her white pinafore, raised their glasses, and Dr Mavor spoke again, above an *obbligato* from Cormack:

She is handsome, she is pretty.
She is the girl of the Golden City.
She is courting one, two, three.
Please to tell me, who is he?

Cormack had his own motives, but they clapped and she beamed, knowing that somewhere down there, in the gas-shadowed streets, thousands of bairns were out playing peevers, splashing through puddles, dancing stand-in-a-ring games, skipping, cowboying and injuning:

It's the Sioux!
They're on the warpath
The nioux!

Hundreds were even now singing and dancing versions of all the rhymes, under billowing washing, in chalked streets. Forty years later, caught by another quartet's performance on a new record-player, Muir even convinced himself – momentarily – they would always do so.

There was only one 'incident'. In the middle of the third movement, an extended, melancholy *lied*, there occurs a mundane, even slightly bawdy, little march: the band plays '*Prinzengarde*', carnival-mocking the pompous, peruked, scarlet-tunicked, tight-white-breeched soldiers, an echo of 1848, something that later builds into a great radical hymn, a wordless version of Beethoven's ninth.

But a bell tinkled.

Muir came back from the ticker-tape machine to say that Emily was delayed in Manchester.

Tomorrow was another working day and they scattered an hour later. Helena left with Mavor and Cormack on the tram to Waterloo Street. But two hours later, changed and concealed by a full, dark dress and mourning veil, she walked back to Park Terrace, and the street-door, unlatched, opened to her touch.

Two hundred miles south Emily was smoking cigarettes with Eva Gore-Booth and her Esther, all warming bare legs as their stockings dried before a log fire in respectable Rusholme. Their conference had become a demonstration in a muddy street, and pretty rough.

'"My grand Whig wife . . . as HE sometimes says." 'A parcel of books daily from Mudies, and a bottle of brandy.' Emily stretched and smiled, 'Aunt Milnes-Gaskell nailed me: a Kantian respect for truth, and an unsparing application of it.'

Lady Emily Muir, born Watson Gordon, was in middle-age handsome rather than winsome, but practical and learned. In 1890 she had enchanted Muir – 'gather our pleasures into a ball' – as they met at a stupefying house-party in a Highland castle.

'We got together and found something to do that didn't involve slaughtering small animals or billiards with bores, but knowing the secret passages of such places . . . the ins and outs. Six months later – 'before he got me pregnant' – we married in the Cathedral.'

The Watson-Gordon flat-fronted grey-stone houses: good Raeburns sharing walls with stags and terriers and ladylike daubs of the Pyramids; clutches of poor relatives roosting like bats in attic and stable. The morality of two centuries before.

Eva and Emily were educated without school though Emily got to Art College. 'I bankroll the laboratory at Dumbarton and the Muir Room at Kelvingrove, queen it at Head Office crushes and launches.' She lit a cheroot and drank off a brandy – not utterly approved of by Esther, but then poor dab she had lost her only child, dead of meningitis at six, and found she couldn't have another.

'Until through young Westermain, I found the automobile, general sobriety, and Robbie, my remarkable Member for the Banff Burghs.'

They had all known Sir Robbie Rattray and his Anna: a Flashman granddaughter who had inherited something from her foul father Eddie and was now in an institution. Robbie had come straight from a byre with some animal magnetism and had carved out an empire from beef. Eva looked thoughtfully at the ceiling.

'He squires me about, goes discreetly to Italy when I do. Esther . . . he knows your George MacDonald, from Huntly! The complaisant lover, but Thank Heavens!'

And from there in her robust way Emily speculated on Mrs Catherine Aitchison, *nee* Reid. Twin daughter of the President of the Royal Scottish Academy: 'That's one of *his*, y'know, from his Sligo days.'

She gestured towards one of the paintings on the parlour wall and that 'Two Japanese Girls' that later became famous.

Eva, slight and very Irish hazarded, 'She's more-than-nice, isn't Catherine? Oughtn't to be the bored wife of a Hogarth officer. Progressive and all that, and a Fabian Lady.'

They discussed this potential compensation for Dr Duncan . . . 'As an arrangement, it might be the best thing in the circumstances. You can't, no matter how hard you try, get engine-dirt out from under my man's fingernails.'

'But Cathy, not Connie. NEVER Connie. That *would* be a step too far . . .'

July 1912, Schottenhaus, Schwarzwald

With a clattering of brakes and gears and pinions, shrieks of steam, a little train pushed its way out of the mist and clambered on to the pale yellow-green of the morning meadow. Below it was industry, clustered in the deep valley under its daft castle, in a clammy, correct grey town. People in white shirts and black coats and skirts slotted into trams and cafes and offices. Up here, seen from the bright meadow, range after range of pine trees, crisp as photographs, marched south.

Her young man Bert, in his worn fawn Norfolk jacket, helped Frieda down from a carriage, then the train chuffed away along its black oily cogwheel track, bearing the respectable to the sunlit tedium of the Grand Hotel Doull. They shouldered their rucksacks and climbed up the green road from the station, paused to consult *Baedeker's Rhine* at the road-end below the few cottages of Lauterbach, then tackled the steep slope to what had been the Almhutte on its shoulder of meadow. At that exotic, fiercely-gabled house, someone had seen them.

'That's them.' Matthias pulled on his shirt. Constance Reid still sprawled her brown length on the feather-bed like some Venusberg harpy.

'They may be progressive, but we have to look decent.'

No-one had come there for years, to its tiny dark bedrooms and grey mattresses, but them; not to labour like the old Catholic *Kleinbauer*, but for sun and fun in summer and sun and snow in winter.

Inside it was dark and cool. Earlier they had opened the shutters and made love in the warm, scented air that rushed in from the meadow. Now, on the balcony, all was ready for the guests. The papers – *Simplicissimus*, whose cartoons seemed to be backtracking on its pacifism – and the *Neue Zuercher Zeitung*. For Matti more important were bottles of red Lemberger wine, Schwarzwaelder ham, broetchen from the village bakehouse, soft Italian cheese, strong old Allgau-Emmentaler, a chutney of apples, quince and pears.

Water swirled from the wooden pipe into a glass jug. Then the sound of voices and boots on the wooden stairs.

'*Frieda und Bert, Gruess dich!*'

'We made that look pretty stupid.'

Constance Reid wiped her mouth with the gingham napkin. Frieda nodded agreement. Her young man remained diffident.

'Eat, drink and be merry, for tomorrow . . .'

'What happens then?' asked Bert.

'We save the world with our CONFERENCE.' Con's face darkened a little.

'And if we don't?'

Matti gave his dry laugh. 'War. Tourism will go down. As will banking. There will be openings for competent mercenaries. Probably not for hotel staff. And how fortunate that my father kept his shares in the Oerlikon factory.'

'Rationalist bastard.' qualified Con.

'That's what we Swiss are. But you depend on us to patrol the battlefields with our red crosses and stop you making even bigger bastards of yourselves.'

'Hypocrite.'

Bert said nothing, but his brown eyes switched from face to eager face. Matti didn't read novels, hadn't heard of him. Con most certainly had.

'I read your *White Peacock*. I loved it, perhaps rather too much.'

He looked at her, mischievous, terrier-like, 'Too Ruskinian? Too many glowing passages?' In that broad Midland voice.

'Could be. I kept wanting your man to run out of words.'

'Silence, then embraces, 'eaving limbs and all that?' She sensed the assumption of daring, reflected almost aggressively. 'How, then, do you write about *that*?'

'Without it sounding either obscene or terribly sentimental? That's really difficult. My first serious girl was a fullhearted lover, talked with her body. Then when we were spent, she said "That was ever so nice." I might have been a big slaice of shop-cake.'

'Obviously not Frieda.'

'Ah, *die Preussenin*.' He glanced coolly along table and balcony to where Frieda and Matthias were looking through a portfolio. 'She didn't regard England as nice in any way.'

'You aren't scandalised?'

'I didn't much like it myself.'

She remembered a ponderous City fiancé. Then Bert nearly shouted 'Though you can respect the BIG DICKENSIAN style. D'you read Wells?'

'Not quite "Can't stand him," but I don't like being taken for granted, a little fluttering woman in the great man's system.'

'You've a point. But I'm not a man for systems anyway. . . . Which is why we're on the run from them. Over the hills and far away.'

She looked along the balcony. Frieda was gazing cat-like at her own diffident man.

'Which means east to Munich, then south to the Tegernsee and over the Alps to Innsbruck. Then to Italy.'

Frieda came back to the table. 'Bert's more German than he says, even if by marriage. But my lot were the real thing. The Richthofens were born with breastplates.'

'Even the women?'

'They were the role models. Valkyrie. What my kid cousin wants to be.'

Bert smiled to himself abstractedly, 'But on a Fokker, not a horse.'

'Eh?'

'It's a Dutch airplane. Moves at forty times the speed of the infantry, spraying death. You're Scotch, aren't you, Constance?'

'Yes, though I've been here since I left Art School.'

'Mystical Scotch? Mechanical Scotch?

'Mystical I hope. My father paints.'

'*Sir* Malcolm Reid.' Bert came back sharply, 'Started as grim realist, followed Courbet. Has moved on. Portraits: politicians, philanthropists, shipbuilders . . . like your sister's great crush?'

'How . . . ?'

'How did I find out about literary Dr Muir? I read the *Bookman*, where the Scotch sport and play, going here and there on their yachts. The Rev Robertson Nicoll tells us everything important: money, holidays, contracts, and as much about the heart or loins of Mr Barrie or Mrs Swan as we need to know.'

At this interesting point Frieda interjected, tapping her watch, 'We have to go leave this earthly paradise quite soon, to get the Munich connection.'

Matti followed, clutching his plans. 'But first, the Work. . . . You'll see the Work?'

Con assented, slightly sulkily. She wanted to rest after the heavy meal, and perhaps make love again, quietly and taking time. But, as the Lawrences saw, after climbing down from balcony to meadow, the Work was arresting enough.

It had preoccupied Matti and Connie all summer. They had met as art-and-science students – industrial designers – hundreds of miles away at the Glasgow Art School, become lovers and socialists in a matter-of-fact way: art students, like gipsies, were allowed this element of bohemianism, even in Glasgow. Then, contracts being thin after the 1908 downturn, they had come back, close to his place, and a commission to paint murals for the restaurant in the new Karlsruhe station. They had found the Almhutte on a summer ramble and, after visiting Wassily Kandinsky and Gabriele Munter in their *Russenhaus* at Murnau, saw its possibilities. The living part was small, but behind it reared the great gable of a dusty *Scheune*, containing the dry bones of old carts and sleds. Out of these they had fashioned a roughly-movable platform, and they used it to paint on the gable their Vita Nuova.

Almhutte became *Schottenhaus*. And Schotten cavorted all across it – robed, naked, kilted – in whirling, dancing, vortices: a mixture of worship, coupling and rhythmic pulses: the battle of life and death: Life embracing her lover, naked in the stream, Death, arrogant-eyed, summoning ranks of swords and bayonets. Spires and minarets versus furnaces and railways and guns. And so on.

'*Wuenderbar*!'

Frieda, gazing up at Con as earth-mother, all bosom and thighs, was effusive, Bert polite:

'Touches of Walt Whitman? Lots of Nietzsche? Futurismo?'

But in 1912 the time had come and the Lawrences went down the green path and into the woods. They would walk to Rossbach and get the train south. Were they impressed? Did they impress?

'I liked him. He has no side.' said Con.

'She propositioned me.' said Matti, 'A quickie in the barn?'

'So much for a repayment of our hospitality. So much for *noblesse oblige*. Bitch.'

'I exaggerate. But there was an element of the come-on. Hand laid on fervent hand. Anyhow, Con, you're beautiful when you're angry.'

'Oldest come-on in the book. Slug.'

'Look, you're stiff with lust. Tart.'

He meditatively untied the drawstring of her shirt, but she pushed him away.

'We're here to be useful, not sensual. This hospitality has got in the way. We still have to do our agenda, get all these people from Godnosewhere into the hotel. Stop the Germans flouncing off because no-one's punched their tickets. Stop the Russians killing each other and the South Slavs killing everyone else. Draft the conclusions before we start. Remember that, sweetie.'

'See that the delegates have soap.'

'See that the British comrades don't call all the women "Love."'

'See that you have a room I can slip in and out of without anyone noticing.'

'See that you don't forget your Dreadnoughts, my boy.'

But the afternoon was hot, the wine had worked, Eros had precedence.

'What have you in mind, Doctor Duerr?'

They kissed for a very long time, he unhooked her belt, she eased her shirt off. Naked to the waist, and remarkably brown, she embraced a lover who . . . had sunburn that ended abruptly at the throat and elbows. The rest of his body was pinky-grey white, not enhanced by tangles of brown hair.

Yet they brought rugs onto the meadow, half-rolled out of the *hutte*, giggling and shivering with desire, scattering myriads of chirupping insects, and made love for a bit, though not for very long, and he was hang-dog.

'I'm sorry. All this . . . *politik* kills my virility. Despite you are so beautiful. And we have so little time before the bloody war. What is there to do but fuck until we drop dead?'

'Don't be morbid. Sweetie, you will live because you're Swiss and are parasitic on every sort of human activity. You call it *verkehr*, intercourse, transport – a branch line of your damn federal railway. How banal can sex get? I because I'm an *ueberlebenskunstlerin*, a survival artist, the only one the Brits care about. . . . What a word! Otherwise we've wasted half an hour. I can't get enough of love, but *liebestod* is off limits.'

And, they reflected, looking down on their discarded clothes, the crushed field-flowers below and around them, the obliging mountains lifting up their heads, the little hills dancing and being glad, and so on, that carnality was still great fun. Saving the world was great fun.

'Naked all-in wrestling!' and they fell back tangled on the rugs.

Matti gazed up into the clear blue, and then at Connie's brown shoulders and pert breasts; his tongue ran over her throat, to the tip of her shoulders.

'Your breasts are brown. And all over . . . Why?'

He was used to Zurich girls whose glories were promoted by careful corsetry, leaving pink weals on their pale flesh. 'Down there' being a triangle of gold between rather large thighs. Con was quite different, with her slim waist, muscled limbs, a tangle of dark hair.

'It's not the sun. I *am* partly Gypsy. And it's Ascona.'

'Ascona . . .' he rather resented that name.

'Ah . . . Lugano without *geld* or inhibitions or clothes.'

'Great in summer. What did you do in winter?

'We did it inside, or went to conferences.'

'Eh?'

'They're Germanic, they may be socialists *aber wir kriegen Ordnung*. So I was a Social-Democrat nudist. There were others, more fun, mainly anarchists. But there were also National Nudists, who worshipped the Body of the Blond Beast. These I didn't like.'

'But I like you enough to give you a second chance. Here.' Then, 'That's it. Right, now stick it in.'

Though stimulated, he still tensed. Con's sexual rationalism nearly unmanned him. Somewhere below them, cowbells clunked. Not a soul was out on the Alm road. He slipped almost out of her thighs and thrust back . . .

'Into your honeypot, my love, into your yoni, your pussy, *deine süsse kleine Muschi.*'

'Can't get enough of phallic tenderness, can we? That's what Bert says. I worry though. People do it all the time, and they love it and each other. But does it change them? Someone says make war not love, and they rape and kill.'

'Worry on. Doing it with someone you love, and without notions of power, is a sort of paradise. Our Greeks forgot that.'

Con reflected on those strange plinths in the Athens Museum they'd visited. The great teachers: topped with a bust then, under the inscription, a flaccid cock extruding itself through the smooth stone. Oddly juxtaposed with the present sense of being cradled by a comfortable male body, with outside, her bare feet and the resilient, painful, regiments of haulms in the mown meadow that could stab her feet between here and there: being naked, tiny, vulnerable in the middle of this Wagner landscape. Then he stopped her mouth with kisses, and this time more confidently. She jabbed her fingers into his back.

'You may be Swiss and mercenary, but you're my lovely lover. I enjoy every moment, every inch. Just carry on doing what you're doing. . . . Don't ever stop.'

Spring 1912: the Clyde

What happened to Miss Mann later that evening, when she returned to the Park flat? Nothing risqué or spectacular, though remarks of Dr Muir, in introduction, suggested otherwise:

'Oh, oh, oh what a whopper! I've never seen one as big as that before!'

'Eh?'

'Marie Lloyd? Hmmm? The vegetable marrow song? Oh forget it!'

'Fourteen-inch.'

'Is that a fact?'

'You aren't mindless with terror?'

Muir had discovered cinematography. He had a side-interest in a Hyndland cinema. On his own screen, sharp-edged in pale grey, a huge gun wheeled below the complicated bridge of the latest Dreadnought, black smoke pouring from its funnels, Goatfell in the background. Clips followed from the Russo-Japanese war of eight years back. The battle of Tsu-Shima. Thousands killed in minutes.

'The way of the Clyde's world, and I wish it weren't.'

Helena tut-tutted. Muir went on,

'I am trying to sell this place cheap, high-efficiency power, which it needs to compete commercially – and it actually benefits your people in Germany. You have the diesel patents. But when the alternative is an arms race, with each new capital ship capable of sinking the last one? On lovely cost-plus contracts?

'Six years ago we were on four eleven-inch guns per ship. Then came the Cawdor Programme and the Dreadnought and things went crazy. Nelson's 'Victory' was forty years old at Trafalgar. *That thing* – Wullie Beardmore's 'Conqueror' – has ten thirteen-point-fives. She's no commissioned yet and already she's obsolete!'

Being summoned back to a tete a tete didn't mean forbidden delight, then.

'You know Bergius and Ballin. You're going back to Berlin. Get it into Ballin's skull that Tirpitz & Co., are at the end of their Latin, as you put it. We don't really need these boats, and you'll be ruined trying to outbuild us.'

'My God! What kind of assignment is that?'

'Think of the last elections. Your Sozis are now the biggest party in the Reichstag. And you know what things are like here.'

Enough folk would write of that advancing, politicised weather: sunlight, stillness, heat – though Miss Mann had so far found the Firth of Clyde far remote in character from cricket-fields, shadowed quadrangles, honey still for tea, etc. Only in good weather and from certain angles had the upper Firth glittered, when the tides off the Tail o' the Bank had dispersed the chemical brown soup that drifted westwards from the Lanarkshire foundries and factories. Otherwise the bare slopes of its surrounding hills held purposive streets of tenements marching out of equally purposive towns. Up close these smelt and smoked, and rang with the noise of the movement of a million-and-a-half workers: tackety-booted, foul-mouthed, dressed in auld claes, smokin' like lums.

The minority – maybe a tenth – of respectable bourgeois sunned themselves to the south-west, as they had always done, in pepperpot-turreted to half-timbered villas surrounded by aspiring shrubs and interspersed with the cropped turf of golf-courses. A few of them had motor-cars in their drives. The grander and older had stables and horses for carriages. To their north-east the proletarian majority faced the concentration of smoke from hundreds of works' chimneys, thousands of tenements, the coal-dust pouring from the chutes of Ardrossan and Govan Quay and the railways that fed them: this spread itself eastwards, over the clotted *mietkaserne*, genteeler housing for skilled workers and a mixter-maxter of tiny industries and retailers, board-schools, hospitals, poorhouses, kirks and chapels, huge graveyards, grand flaring bars – strung out along the electric trams.

A federated urbanism – what a century before, the novelist John Galt had christened 'the West' – was punctuated by green islands of public parks and shaggier, though irregular, stretches of older forest. Behind much of it swelled great, bald, dark moorland, small colliery towns adrift upon it, plugged by mineral railways into international commerce, and after 1900 open to political change. New and less couthy tones gave voice to the General Council of the Scottish Miners' Union. James Keir Hardie 'Myner Collier', shaggy socialist, had captured it 1909, and in 1914 seemed less mystic and more menacing.

Even if, in some of the villas, and at Italianate Portencross, south of the steamer station at Wemyss Bay, he was welcome as another guest of Dr Duncan Muir, shipyard director, Liberal MP for North Renfrew, styled the 'socialist millionaire', a distortion of both words, but reassuring.

That was Helena Mann summing up: surveying Stothers's *Glasgow and West of Scotland Annual* before the gas fire in her digs near Byres Road Subway, along with a six-inch map. The pale blue of the Clyde ran into it like scissors cutting cloth, north and south were complex brown hatchings, green for woods, red for major roads; isolated small groupings of black squares representing houses. The *Annual* she used to fill this in with stiff formal portraits, views of country houses or council buildings, new trains, steamers being launched. The people snapped there exuded respectability: kirk ministers, ironmasters, footballers, advocates. Were they a potential arsenal? Or were they a power for peace?

That had been her friends' remit in the *Auslandsabteilung* of the Berlin Marine Office. Einkreisung – 'Encirclement' was the situation: the suspicion-to-certainty that in the event of a war with France, Britain would take the side of the French. If so, what resources could the Clyde throw into this?

Espionage? Not strictly, at this stage. Helena was *Anglistin*, studied contemporary history – at Berlin University. Maybe 'reasons of state' had got her the grant, but from a 'peace party' around the German shipping millionaire Albert Ballin. A pacific Glasgow? Way-out in terms of possibility, they reckoned, but it might play. Scottish Lord Haldane had come to Berlin that February, and wanted to talk peace. Ballin was Jewish, got on well with the Social Democrats. Could she come up with stuff, contacts, something that moderates could use? Calculations of the resources of the peace party, and so on?

She had gone with a letter of introduction to Muir from the engineer Bergius, who had been at Charlottenburg with her father. *'Sehr nett Mensch, treibt die Musik, heiratet mit eine Drachenin, aber eine freundliche Drachenin.* 'Muir, married to a friendly dragon, Lady Emily: on Helena's mantlepiece, under a vast hat, she addressed a Liberal gathering. She had rapidly settled Helena in the large spare room of a widow of a Portencross gardener, in a curious little rural enclave almost completely surrounded by four-storey tenements, with a small stables, greenhouses and a slightly discouraged-looking market garden.

For months she had gone to sleep with, and been wakened by, the sounds of the countryside in the city: the whinny of ponies, crooning of pigeons, 'scrake of dawn' from seabirds mobbing in the cobble streets. These held the trams, the steam-whistles, at bay. Helena, from her fresh-painted Berlin suburb, ventured out into this strange, dishevelled place. She took full advantage of being 'furrin' when natives launched into elaborate narratives about politics or family (semi-comprehensible), religion and football (stay away). Then literature (read, listen, learn) and then art. Pace the floors of that vast Kelvingrove gallery, centred in the limitless living gallery of the city. But to what result?

On the Royal Scot 28th June

Duncan Muir's career as MP was nominal, aided by a secure pairing with a Cambridge Tory friend. His elder brother Sir Henry, second Baronet, was a junior minister. In early June 1914 he had to finish the Economy Committee's report on the Research Department, but was called back to the Borders. At Alderwood the chief of the clan, Uncle Aeneas (82) was dying: sickroom was relentlessly modulating into deathbed. Duncan would have to go in Henry's stead; but he prepared to slip south in some style.

He boarded the Glasgow-London 'Royal Scot' at Carstairs from the Peebles local, hoping for tranquillity, a good meal and bottle of wine, cigars and a reflective pipe. In London a conversation with Cathy Aitchison, née Reid waited, whose charm and verve chafed under near-widowhood in a Cathcart villa . . . or was her sister Constance the fairer (certainly the more dangerous) of the two? His thoughts were interrupted by a familiar voice.

'Muir, I have been lookin' for you. Lunch with me. You can't refuse.'

In the massive and famously stable twelve-wheel dining car, Quentin Kennedy, Lord Westermain, MP, lay in wait. The good news was that Muir would have had to see him anyway; the bad that his intellectual enchantment, from friendly to far-fetched, would last until Preston.

The mythology that would accumulate around Westermain (the title was a courtesy) was in the future. He was then the Liberal heir to the Marquess of Kintyre, who owned most of South Wales and a huge castle on the Clyde. Like Winston Churchill, fifteen years older, he was reckoned 'a faddist but running on some horsepower', toying with various semi-socialistic enthusiasms, liberal Catholicism, the Scottish Home Rule Association, the Territorial Army. In the eyes of Chief Whip Adam, a good judge of men, he was 'a handful'.

Westermain wasn't much younger than Muir, but still appeared as an earnest youth with carrotty hair and matching moustache at the bottom of a long nose which, with close-set, bespectacled eyes, made him look like a thoughtful horse. This added to a reputation for enthusiasms, which he carefully indulged. Before he spoke in earnest, he tended to narrow his eyes, and having dabbed the last of the soup from his lips, he now did.

'Muir, you are through Cavaliero wired into that culture of moral and social innovation loosely called 'Futurist' – are you not?'

Muir nodded.

'Generated by those young fellows in Glasgow who call themselves the Scots *avant-garde* (when they're not drinking) scientific-artistic humanists, etc.: Walter Elliot, John Grierson – no more than a student – Osborne Mavor, Boyd Orr?

'Yes.'

'All much influenced by Shaw, Bergson, Pat Geddes and the 'life-force'. Which may give our own encounter – 'wild' coincidence – some historical form. Pity your Emily isn't here to take minutes.'

Muir sighed inwardly for a tranquillity now vanishing into the surrounding hills. An earlier train journey to Cambridge had Westermain boiling on about economics, publishing and literary piracy in the USA and its links to the militant Irish nationalism of Sinn Fein. They had talked without break for four hours, never uninterestingly. The present conversation was going to be even less related to ordinary political chat. But then again, Westermain was no ordinary politician.

Cumberland rumbled past, Eden Valley, Penrith – mountains to the west; then there would be Carnforth and the broad bleak sands over which stagecoaches had once splashed to the Lakes, then Lancaster and Preston, where Westermain would alight for Peveril, vast Pugin-Gothic house of his Catholic cousinhood.

'How're you copin' with your Ulstermen, Muir?' he queried,

'Does this confirm your readin' of the runes last time: top of the market, top of the tide? Harland and Wolff shiftin' to the Clyde, drums, flutes and all? How'll you cope with the dour Proddie men from the Shankhill? – Belfast on the inland sea, not Ireland?'

Muir, engineer to trade, held to these conversations because Westermain expeditiously did his thinking for him.

'I picked up your argument that time about Catholic Ireland really being peculiar in its fundamental resistance.' he offered. 'Its elite regarding pirate publishing in America as deserved revenge.'

'Far more effective than Fenian guns.' Westermain responded, 'Fits into my ideas about the natural – national – history of mercantilism. Irish-American-German-Hungarian. Comes from our Jacobite econo-mist Stuart of Coltness (more read than Adam Smith, remember!) via

Hamilton and Henry Carey in America and Hegel and List in Germany to Deak in Hungary. In our own day Parnell and Griffith in Ireland. We British are further than ever from the Irish, but not for the usual reasons.'

Such retarding data was necessary, otherwise the constructions and comparisons would pour out and out and on and on. Yet his notion of innovation in Ireland made sense. Against: the place's disastrous economic history. For: Henry Ford's car, Thomas Holland's submarine, Marconi. Westermain had books and pamphlets and tracts to hand: an attaché-case full of them.

Conversation was suspended as a commotion broke out in the Dining Saloon: four energetic, very drunk artisans who at Penrith had capered on to this grand stage from a Whitehaven train: paid off from what steamer, from where?

A causerie was slipping forward on vituperative obscenity, like high-pressure steam:

'You consider that fucking working, yak hunt? Fucking liners is poof's work. Ah've just done five fucking months on coal – Swansea tae Piraeus, then ontae Odessa wi' cotton, an' grain back.'

Then . . .

'AH KEN HIM!'

Oh Christ, let it pass!

'Yon's DOCTOR DUNCAN MUIR. Ye piss-artist!'

As if attempting to stem this torrent, Westermain, ever rational, resumed to Muir:

'If one is Irish, even by inclination rather than race, one tends to speculate on the byways: not the obvious or orthodox, but families, genius, unorthodox notions.'

He gazed – not at fulminating humanity, possibly knuckling itself against him – but at the lincrusta ceiling of the carriage. He smiled, almost to himself – reminding Muir why he was called Moriarty at Cambridge. Even more arcana followed:

'The reason I drew your attention to your young Glasgow friends is that I have on my conscience a young man called Robertson. Obsessed with airplanes. Not orthodox scientific but he has got himself on to a very big issue – you as a shipbuilder should be concerned with it. Replacing coal with oil. Something our officials have missed. He has been round the labs to tap experts. Some of them are on the trail.'

'Quentin Westermain is like an otter,' H G Wells had told him, 'his teeth lock on impact' and rehearsed the remainder of the conversation for pillow-talk with Cathy Aitchison later that evening: 'He gets a Big Idea every two years, and batters away with it so that some of it will lodge even in the average politician's brain. We live in a world where experts produce specialisms that don't co-operate, yet still tout themselves as universals. Quentin and his protégé think our present coal economy is *finito*.'

Westermain's idealism waxed as the train laboured over Shap Summit, saw the Lune Gorge drop away to the left:

'. . . Think about what a war might do to innovation. Big-scale air could work out cheaper, safer and more manageable than sea. First for passengers, then for high-grade freight, if war doesn't impose its own priorities. . . . All this comes from an almost complete outsider, though Edgeworth at Cambridge (whom I've discussed this with) has some notion of making him a sort of research fellow.'

Muir tried hard to brake him:

'My people aren't so optimistic. Glasgow economists think that oil is a false trail. Still needs subsidy, not tied to the winch of escalating coal demand. I tried to convert the output of our biggest refinery – Pumpherston – to coal-equivalent: net output only of a small coalfield. And look at West Lothian. Damn red mountains of waste-shale.'

There came from further along the carriage:

'Look, you're no makin' sense, ye wee shite – but ye're no' even a shite, ye're jist a wee toalie – ye know fuck aa' aboot keeping the boats o' Doctor Muir fuckin' afloat. Gaes oan an' oan aboot aa' his socialist ideas but there's somethin' ahint it. Ten year ago a wis at the wheel o' the *Nan Shan* three days oot o' Hong Kong an' we hits a wall o' water. Auld MacWhirr wis supposed tae be in charge but he wis too donnert. His mate had fuckin' gave up. The waves were brakin' oan the bridge an' the funnel near-awa, but she stays under control. Muir's boat.'

'Imagine the envelope, man, eh?' Westermain came back:

'The 'Titanic' was 50,000 tons: two hundred per passenger. Imagine doing that for 500 passengers at five times the speed with a crew of five! Robertson says our air technology is still like the atmospheric steam engine before James Watt started on it, let alone Elder or Kelvin: size of a house – and feeeble!'

'Airships?'

'Not necessarily. No reason why we can't have very big planes with four, maybe eight, engines.'

Westermain on Robertson on new applications of turbines – to flight technologies – based on a day spent in the Voith Works at Heidenheim. Robertson predicting that we would be in a bad way if we persisted with battleships and liners, citing a Kipling story about airships he, Muir, had never managed to finish, let alone understand.

'. . . The thinking military reckon that the proportion of world shipping vulnerable to submarines will rise from 10% to 50 % within the next five years. Frightening when you compare the *Financial Times* stuff on insurance cover! On the other hand it could provide cash for new technology which may – just – be about to cohere. What do you know of aircraft in the Balkan Wars? Damn all, I imagine, but . . .'

Then the words Muir feared above all . . .

'Erra perra' em, ower therr . . .'

But Westermain strode over to their table.

'Look, my friend, from what I have heard you may have a legitimate case.' He said. 'But you are drunk and failing to make very much sense. You will shortly become offensive and probably incontinent as well, and shame yourself. If you are sensible you will desist while you are still on the moral high ground.'

The very large man stopped.

'Y'know, you may have a point.'

'Never discount someone who has been around.'

Doors swung open, the riotous party descended at Lancaster.

'Where were we?' asked Westermain.

'Are you going to get this from the Admiralty? You are not. This is coming from young Robertson: Albino, thus near-blind, possessed by his specialism to the point of mania, who lives from hand to mouth in a hovel and can't write for toffee. His bright sister (who can) is chronically ill. Some French academic – Durkheim, Halbwachs? – said that the Celts nurtured such folk within their clans.'

'. . . And the only weapon you can use against a sub is a plane.'

Westermain descended at Preston. An hour later at Crewe a recuperated Muir, enjoying a second bottle of claret with a pipe of Dr White, realised that something else had gone wrong.

'Injin's fell oot.' said the waiter.

Muir filled his pipe again, got out onto the hot, suncaked platform and since the first class diner was near the head of the train, walked up to the stricken, elegant black beast. It was named 'Sir Gilbert Claughton' on a red-and-brass plate: suggesting a director in a big dull house in Cheshire. A squad of mechanics crawled about the spartan cab and what they called the 'running gear'. He could see the fundamental connections with his own trade: the components could be taken apart, rejigged, and used to drive a ship. But with diesels his works were off in a different direction, towards power-stations, control rooms, electrics. Westermain was probably right. This was an antique.

A fitter was phoning from the head of the platform:

'Centre bearing's going red-hot. They've never mastered that problem with compounds. Find a new loco at the works? How long?'

He grimaced at Muir, and a fair-faced premium apprentice who was standing by.

'Maybe twenty minutes, if . . .'

He could see his London schedule unravelling, especially that important hour-and-a-half with Cathy before they turned up for the Russian ballet at the Coliseum. It drove him back to the dining car and Westermain's files. And, in a more general way, to the latter's alarming thought-sequence. Here was the most powerful locomotive of the British Empire's wealthiest railway, sick with a fundamental malady of design.

What was that line of Blake's? 'The invisible worm, that flies in the night, has conquered your bed, oh rose.' The parallel seemed at first as dotty as Blake. But think: out of the London Blakeians had come Sidney Gilchrist Thomas, who invented the mass-production of non-phosphoric steel. Taken up by the Germans, it had in thirty years got them where they were now . . . how could Britain compete?

Westermain didn't just get to him via Westminster. At Dumbarton he'd paired his Robertson with another associate, Strobelius: a Polish electrical engineer; reckoned his ideas might work. The pair had refined them into *Dalriada* a thirty-foot sloop, now with a diesel engine: convincing enough to win over some offhand backing from Winston at the Board of Trade, but Muir's Committee experience left him more impressed with Lloyd George at the Exchequer.

'So, Doctor Muir,' Westermain had concluded, as the train braked for Preston, 'a triflin' dollop from you would enable the above lot to help Robertson to register his main patents and work on the other 'carrier' prototype. I want to help in any way I can. At worst, it could protect our ships from notional German U-Boats in the North Sea and off the Atlantic coast . . . cost of radio stations set off against secure grain supplies, *et cetera*.'

Westermain was already years ahead. Muir had earlier wondered how realistic the whole thing was. Now that his own chick the *Dalriada* had run the 'measured mile' part of his own gamble was in play.

Suffolk, 3 August, Flying Chancellor

The Lord Chancellor of England, a Scot, was presently covering the War Ministry; Jack Seely had retired hurt from the Irish crisis. Viscount Haldane of Cloan had turned out in a heavy knickerbocker suit of dark-green corduroy. He did not 'do' informality and had not relished the stifling weather, or the long dusty trip to the fringes of London in a closed War Office car. Perspiration trickled off the famous domed head. But if he was scared Richard Burdon Haldane, Viscount Haldane of Cloan, was determined not to show it, least of all to the young men in grimy overalls who clustered round the aircraft. 'Engine's a 60 horse-power Panhard-Levasseur.' whispered the red-tabbed Incroyable from the dicky-seat, sensing that a challenge would shortly come from the overalls, and trying to talk the alien speech. The Minister gave him a withering look.

'Goethe made himself climb to the top of Strasbourg tower, in 1789. The readiness is all.'

He beamed comprehensively at those around him. They beamed back. A sergeant hurried up with overalls, clean and white this time and a flight jacket.

'It gets very cold.'

Haldane was installed in the poky aft cockpit – the texture of the hot leather, the banana oil and its narcotic smell would stay with him for the rest of his life, and the pilot hoisted himself up ahead. A sort of aircraft groom ran round to the machine's head, swung on the wooden propeller which was its sole elegance

Thwuck . . . Thwuck . . . ThwuckaThwuckaThwucka – and dashed clear of the circle of frozen speed. The plane lurched forward through a cloud of exhaust, bounced swaying across the grass and as the motor's racket swelled, uneasily took to the air.

Don't look down! Haldane told himself, and seconds later, Do look down! The canal, then the highroad with a farm cart and panicked horses, then field after harvest field, a chocolate and cream train with its blue engine, falling back behind him. He remembered that tale of Kenneth Grahame's – ' "Poop! poop!" cried Toad.'

'Who, for the sake of argument, we shall call Winston Toad.' he added mentally. But he could see how Winston had got bitten: after foetid Capital, car and airfield, the cold air clarified and exhilarated. They climbed to avoid a trailer of cloud which cut off the ground, and across its woolly surface sped their shadow caught by the evening sun. Then the plane banked to the left, and in the corner of his eye he caught the airfield and in its right-hand corner the tiny shapes of three or four other planes.

A larger and less friendly cloud loomed up at ten o' clock, dense and looking like a cathedral of whipped cream. The aeroplane steered to the right though for a minute or so it was caught by one of its buttresses and even the wing-tip vanished in the white. Then out again and below them a suburb – villas, church, cemetery, a big official-looking building: hospital? poorhouse? Momentarily he glimpsed the skirmishing force down there: taking cover behind the hedges, advancing grave-by-grave through the cemetery. Haldane remembered earlier days: the staff-car edging along the lanes, the pok-pok-pok of blank rounds, bank-manager Territorial captains touchy about their out-of-uniform status. 'There is only one thing worse than obeying an order, and that is giving one.' John Stuart Mill was unhelpful, while for the Germans it would all be cut-and-dried. And now this eye in the sky viewed the battlefield like a map.

Something garbled came through the speaking tube. He couldn't make it out but the pilot was gesturing to the right. Another wall of cloud, immense and livid-flecked. Once inside it, the engine-noise dropped and the air became damp and clammy. The machine stumbled, yawed to the left, jolted back rightwards, fell into clear air and below them was a forest which seemed to stretch on and on. He coughed something sour into his mouth. Would he disgrace himself and throw up? And at once they slipped under the shelf of cloud and found below a broad road between dark pinewoods, along which a black touring-car scurried, trailing ochre dust. The pilot signalled again, this time left, and God be thanked there were bell-tents and horses and khaki figures and a few minutes later, not without bouncing and lurching, they were down. A bearded man in a general's field uniform stepped down from the tourer and shyly grinned.

'Hail the Flying Chancellor.'

'Your Majesty.'

'The Black Stone gang collared! Well done, your chaps, particularly young Hannay. You didn't mind using the plane? MI5 says the Boche might still be tapping phones. So I also have to tell you you're all clear on the Research Department: Arthur Balfour vouches for the Tories.' Land-bound and middle-aged, the pair plodded silently to the airfield periphery in the wake of his car, then

'This isn't just pleasure,' the King said. 'You know more than most about our friends in Berlin. . . . It's not a family quarrel, even though Willie takes so much after his grandmother. Letters to the papers in green ink, with many underlinings. But it's where he is that makes it deadly. You've tried, dear fellow, you've tried. You and Loulou Harcourt and that nice little Jew shipowner.'

Haldane thought of Albert Ballin, his host in Berlin in February 1912 supported by the Democrats and the Left: his model town in the Hamburg docks for emigrants 'Ballinstadt', his reputation among those devils from the Militarkabinett as 'getarnt Sozi . . . judische Dreck' even when he bankrolled them; the way they had parted at the Hamburg-Bahnhof when both of them had failed, and for the gentle people he had dined with the evening before, Cassirer, Kessler, Liebermann. 'Here I stand, I can do no other.' Albert had said, and shrugged his shoulders in a slightly exaggerated way, 'Leb' wohl, Richard, mach's gut.'

'They will fight, sir, and they won't have much to restrain them. You signed the Parliament Act three years ago. William would have stabbed himself rather than do that . . . Our Tories caved in; I doubt whether the Berlin lot will.'

'And what will happen, Haldane?' the king whacked at thistles with his stick. 'Not what you planned on eight years ago, I dare say. Nothing like these things.'

He wagged the stick at the planes. 'Or those huge guns they can use on French fortresses. Douglas Haig tells me this is the long haul. But does he tell the people in the streets, the editors? So bloody. . . .

'And if these things win wars these days, wouldn't we be better to keep the chaps in the factories? And what factories? We haven't got our own Krupps.'

'I don't know, sir, but we can evolve. The Chancellor while at Trade developed a remarkable rapport with engineers and shipbuilders, using our 'technicals', backbenchers like Duncan Muir his "Captains of Industry" he calls them.'

'I know Muir. Married Archie Watson-Gordon's daughter, former Maid of Honour. Is that a recommendation? I expect her Suffragette friends to launch themselves on my car any day now.'

Certainly, Lloyd George had amazed him as much as old Campbell-Bannerman and Asquith

'. . . and the First Lord learns the "shop" of anything like that rapidly. But we do require something closer to a Committee of Public Safety, to handle this militarisation. It's unprecedented.'

He recollected a cheeky nephew comparing the combustible Winston to a Giant Panda: 'Eats, shouts, and leaves!'

'Lloyd George and . . . Churchill? Committees of Public Safety?' Neither prospect seemed to reassure the King.

They came to the field-gate, the staff-car lumbering after them. The dusk was gathering, clammily. Sandringham was a five-hour drive.

2

'Blow, Bugle, Blow!'

In capital and province,
unlikely armourers prepare for battle.

Late August 1914: Imaginary Forces

Duncan Muir, given to the innocent vanity of the powerful and righteous, stared critically into the mirror of the saloon-car, adjusted his soft white collar over his cobalt blue tie, and rang the electric bell for breakfast. At Carlisle Cathy Aitchison left the train and the *Financial Supplement* to the *Herald* joined it. Muir saw her slender, purposeful figure striding along the platform to the Whitehaven train and in due course to her agreeable father at Coniston.

The steward, discretion well-rewarded, served coffee, and buttery rolls. There was haddock and there would later on be kidneys and bacon and scrambled eggs, as he didn't intend to lunch. Colvilles of Motherwell didn't know how to cook even if he was a director. West Coast Joint Stock did. But Colvilles had rolled a new type of steel for the 'Batavia', a strong, lightweight alloy, revolutionary, to go with the rest of the boat.

'Nae funnel?'

'Doesn't need one. Wind resistance, gets in the way. Exhaust goes up the hollow mast.'

'Well, ye're the radical wan.'

Many Clyde shipyards were still set in the steam days of the 1870s. Not so Barclay Curle's German imports: white coats in white workshops. At all points they could squeeze the estimates down. Fewer crew but better paid, better fed. Keir Hardie didn't grudge him that, and he had repaid him. 'Batavia', 'Venetia', 'Helvetia': the Republic class. But would he any longer be the Socialist Millionaire, after yesterday's audience?

Muir was in the modern monastic cell: the sleeping-car berth, thinking lewd thoughts about Cathy Aitchison, elsewhere on the Night Scot. Smiles, an affecting hug, and possible dates for dinner now . . . and the hope of making love there and after making love, switching off and sleeping, unheeding the muffled drumming – of steel on steel. All of this brought – with mixed justification – thoughts of his body cupping hers, treasuring her, and of those smiles and murmurs by which serious lovers set the world to rights.

He tried to rationalise where they'd got to. Not to that stage. At one level, slanting lines of steel, clicking together to form a path to somewhere, a Westermain-Robertson vision of a Jules Verne war-on-war. At another, the possibilities of love. He as Undershaft, she as Major Barbara? The chance that a boring, homicidal male world might be flipped over the edge, and something come out that was sensuous and the discourse released by and around it. The exact words memory struggled with, and then – altogether elsewhere – the context:

> Can this cock-pit hold
> The vasty fields of France? Or may we cram
> Within this wooden O, the very casques
> That did affright the air at Agincourt?
> O pardon: since a crooked figure may
> Attest in little place a million,

And let us, ciphers to this great accompt,
On your imaginary forces work.
Frail travelling coincidence! Cathy was learned enough for Emily,
who had signalled thus, cryptically, before sailing to Buenos Ayres.

'The cerebral sister. A better choice than Connie. wears men like
fancy boots. What's Connie in this crisis for? She'll acquire morality
by and by . . . '

Sir Robbie would be waiting for her at Montevideo. Muir drifted off
into an historic reverie. West of the railway, out in the clay of
Ecclefechan, old Carlyle slept, who saw *Henry V* as 'the English epic',
though the place was 'Eglwys Fach': Welsh for his 'little tabernacle'.
Carlyle the Scot of Scots, named after an English city. Its Scots Bishop
Duncan cursed the Borderers, just as Bishop Douglas translated Virgil
as *Eneados*, finishing only days before king and court fell dead at
Flodden. Crooked figures, millions as small change . . . Burns's pacific
brotherhood   reduced   to   friends   and   brothers   .   .   .
A drunken farmer and the fiends of hell.

'Of Brownyis and Bogillis fule is this buke.'

July 1914: on the 'Dalriada'

A fortnight earlier Sir Duncan's sloop had cleared Portencross Skerries
and smacked into the choppy wave-ridges that came up the Firth on the
edge of a sharp south-westerly. In the clear morning the northern
shoulder of Goatfell on Arran stood out cold, angular.

Dalriada's as old as I am. A present from George L. Watson to my
father on his marriage.'

'George L. who?'

'Famous yacht builder. Died young, like my dad. This boat is my
version of a bike.'

Muir gestured at various ingenious motors and pulleys. The 'bike'
could be single-manned, or driven against tide and wind by its neat
diesel. He whirled the wheel to starboard and the boom snapped over,

allowing the mainsail to scoop the wind. She ran comfortably towards the island.

He grinned and in a complicated movement simultaneously handed Cathy the pay-out for the jib and lit his pipe. Cathy hunkered down in the lee of the snug cockpit, wrapped in a bulky white pullover that smelt of dog and oil, topped by an Aran tammy. And reckoning: if she didn't end what Masefield – once a favourite – called the long trick, she might be in for a dull passage to nowhere in particular.

'Don't you get lonesome at Portencross if your wife is always away preaching to her sisterhood? Though I don't disagree with the cause.' She thought long about that line and chucked it out.

Go on the basis that she was as sexually adept as her twin? Her husband, Hugh had learned something in the orient.

'Nah. Emily has her compensations. I'm a useful token man. Keep myself busy with . . .'

He noted that her cockpit contortion wasn't just comfortable but suggestive, then broke off and pointed at a big freighter to the south, its buff-funnel issuing folds of black smoke. Motionless, it picked up a pilot.

'Replacing these, for a start. Your husband commanded one?'

There was, he gathered, a handsome Bengali widow, with a big chandlery in Madras and notions of a fleet of her own, to preoccupy Captain Hugh. Under free trade, the Indians would be building up their own marine.

'Look!' she shaded her eyes and beckoned to the north.

The wind had carried them some distance up the Firth, the entry to Loch Long to port. She pointed to where against purply-brown hills a pale grey shape stood out. A westerly gust slapped waves against the sloop's prow, and as they approached, the shape formed itself into a Dreadnought.

'HMS Conqueror.'

'One of our Conquerors?' Meredith too, by God.

'Meaning that Beardmore has the say?' she came back.

'Only for the moment. Things will have to change. When they do, small and manoeuvrable will win. Like you, sweetie. Shall we head back to Portencross?'

As she rose from the supper-table, hours later, Browning came to mind . . .

And nobody calls you a fool,
And people suppose me clever.
This could but have happened once . . . ?

They didn't miss it that time. Affinities and bargain clicked into place. That was the end of the theoretical part. The practical briskly followed and both reckoned they passed with flying colours. They came down, gowned like Renaissance consorts, to fruit and liqueurs.

August 1914: Kyles of Bute, on the 'Antelope'

War announced itself through hours-into-days of telegrams and special editions, conferences and journalists smoking their lungs out. *Alea iacta est!* Charlie Masterman, failed Liberal Minister, triumphant propaganda chief, nervously plotted and ployed behind dim generals and admirals who lurched forward they knew not where. The literary ranks were filled up, much indifferent prose and verse churned out – Kipling doubly-patriotic about France – though Hardy was overall gloomy and Conrad, however obliquely, pro-German. All telephone and cable-lines led to Wellington House, an ugly office-block in the Strand.

A young man was sent four hundred miles by express train on the newly-nationalised railway. By a smaller train to a quiet Clyde pier. By a miniature steamboat to Toward Point. The mail-pinnace, having delivered David Paterson, private secretary to the brothers Muir, stringer for the *Scotsman*, along with various bits of bad news, scudded back to Ardrossan.

The yacht *Antelope* drowsed, waves slapped, a feather of white wafted from a slumbering donkey-engine. Yet after some minutes, far-forrard, the donkey heehawed, hissed and clanked, and wound an anchor-chain on board. Freed, 'Antelope' momentarily drifted by the stern. From her smokestack the slow coil of black dispersed, replaced by a purposeful column of heat, in which the Argyll hills quivered. The screw churned and crew scurried about. In the midst of all this, contained in his dark, high-buttoned reefer suit, the world's richest man read the telegrams the little boat had brought, through his gold spectacles. Wraith-like in white, the Hon Charles Harcourt MP danced attendance on the Croesus of Pittsburgh.

'We dock at Birkenhead in eleven hours. By then we ought to have some notion of where the world's headed and can telegraph. Compare this lot with your *Financial Times* and plan to move about a million. Bonds should be stable, might even improve. You tell me where we could do better.'

'Shall I look for equities which will rise with the emergency?'

'Ships? Grain? Not armaments, boy. I have a reputation to think of.'

'The eyes in that sunny pink countenance were blue and remarkably youthful, though beard and hair were white.' Paterson went on to inform his *Scotsman* readers that Mr Innes, Scots-American steelman, was not yet won over to the war. But Masterman had told him to hand over the packet of stuff from the American consul at Liege, and that might change things. The Germans had, in a sense, played by the rules, but the discretion given their commanders had been excessive. Innes was wobbling, though still drawing on the strings of armed neutrality. Belgium was totally Catholic; *that* would play for the Irish and about time too. Folk forgot quite quickly the Congo and ten million dead Africans . . .

. . . 'But we can still push your point about the people of goodwill.

We can cable Shaw and Tagore and Frau von Suettner and send their stuff to Editor Scott at the *Manchester Guardian*.'

The rocks and trees of Argyll were now floating past them. A thousand tons of buff and white steel, the 'Antelope' slipped down the Kyles and into Loch Fyne. To starboard a tiny puffer chugged over a glassy, lazy swell towards Ardrishaig, the Crinan Canal and the Hebrides. To the south-east a three-master lay anchored off Lochranza waiting for a tug. Otherwise the Firth was empty.

But in Berlin and London the decisions – as Paterson later noted – were being made which would within twelve months propel a Turkish torpedo into the *Antelope's* flank and send her and half her crew to decay on the floor of the Aegean.

Somewhere in this was Muir, who had passed the political business on to his brother, and concentrated on 'guiding the emotion into constructive channels . . . To convince, one must take part.' Over weeks, becoming months, he sent clever memos to Whitehall on the Baltic and combined operations, the Dardanelles and ditto (someone four decades later found them, unopened, in the papers of T MacKinnon Wood, Scottish Secretary). Divided between Dumbarton commerce and Whitehall strategy, he put Westermain's young inventor, Robertson, at the test-tank next to the Dumbarton yard. Haldane put him on his Department of Scientific and Industrial Research and found a place for Cathy translating captured German documents. Emily and her Robbie were at the other end of the South American telegraph. Did Asquith notice? Did Kitchener notice?

The 'magnificent poster' remained unmoved.

Barrhead to Wemyss Bay, July 1914

The ILP's socialists were out in some disorder, preaching the Second International's Stuttgart Conference resolutions against the wardrums. After half-a-day's spasmodic leafleting in the high shy street of Barrhead, the Clarioneers had called it quits, pedalled for the summit, and once over it, flung their bikes on the road-verge, and settled for sandwiches and lemonade alfresco on a bluff above the Clyde: one tall and two short girls, and three boys, all the right side of twenty: one fat and two comparatively slim.

'Whit a bunch of eejit bigots. Oh dear, we're shown up as the plaster saints of rationalism,' Bob Cormack, now-passed engineer at Ballantyne Muir, sighed melodramatically. He had not quite held his own at Barrhead High Street against an Orange orator: impenetrably Belfast, armourclad in prejudice:

'Un oor Scoats herts wey bullieve un Democracy an' the Freedom of our Pratestunt Union an' its Marturs. Whan the Umpire stands indanger, Ulstur wull fight furr ut, and Ulstur wull be right! Furr nuthun, but nuthun', can match tha conspiracy thut issa Catlick Churrch, an' thu parvershuns o' the Whoor o' tha Sevan Hulls!'

Brazen lungs had won out over all the isms of Blatchford's *Clarion* and even Tom Johnston's *Forward*. Not just that: the Protestant had the dry rattle of drums, guns and marching men behind him, and a government army whose officers had mutinied at their Curragh Barracks outside Dublin rather than fight them. Things did not look good, in that workaday High Street with its drifts of semi-interested, semi-respectable people.

Then Bob took out his fiddle from its battered case and prepared to pay him back. To the dread basso of Belfast he replied with first a reel – the Foula reel, a foot-tapper – then 'Meriwether Reid's jig' and then, as the audience gathered in curiosity, his ace: 'Carolan's Reply'. This didn't promise any victory of enlightened exchange, but enchanted. It might have been a waltz, danced by revenants to some ghostly Great House, by the Wild Geese and their girls. In the douce world of soirees and weddings at which he played it minded him of Burns's 'Mary Morison' and caught his heart –

Yestreen, when to the trembling string,
The dance gae'd through the lichted ha',
To thee my fancy took its wing,
I stared but neither heard nor saw . . .

Though he glanced at Helena Mann, brown eyes under an ivorine brow, under a check Tam o' Shanter, as he launched out, rewarded by a big, beaming grin. Eternities were in our Bob, and seemed to guide bow and fingers, until he again became Raeburn's Niel Gow, giving out the dance, but captured by a music outside him. The bairns started first to jig, then a young couple, the girl with a wee wean in her shawl, put their arms round each other and danced, and others, first shyly, then more boldly, jined oan. Out of that Saturday crowd, in a town famed for building water-closets, appeared a man with a bodhran, then a piper. Bob struck up a wilder dance. Even the Orangeman, scowling, was tapping his feet . . .

And then the Red Cyclists leaked out of Barrhead, on to their saddles, and into the gentle Renfrewshire hills.

'It's no yir City Parliament, no it's no. But it passes for politics roon' here, mair nor any socialist gospel' concluded Pete Cullen, the plump carriage-builder of St. Rollox. The two smaller girls with rosy cheeks, Pheemie and Maisie, milliners at the Co-op, were really there for looks – but calculating that young engineers were not a bad bet (they could surprise, clerks couldn't) – giggled *unisono*. Watson Wilson, cook, kept himself to himself, as usual, but Pete was vocal,

'Ma Goad, Wattie, wid ye look at this lot: the Chamber o' Commerce's annual photie. A thoosand men in bowlers, every wan wi' a big moustache. No' a beard, a shave nor a wumman amang them. Oor maisters, praying for Christ tae gie them wan original thocht.'

Helena reflected: was it not Fact that this bunch were anything but socialist? Instead of fomenting revolution, were they not looking for older folks' shoes to slip into? For Pheemie the clasp of Pete's hand would signal when solidarity gave way to the oldest conspiracy, for the steady job and two-bedroom flat. Her own people were anyway from outside – mother Scots but father an agent in Manchester for special steels from Essen – and if politics carried on as they'd been doing, she might find herself an exile – or worse. She had also been using her sharp almond eyes and tongue – much appreciated – to explore outside this milieu. Her stipend from the Kaiser-Wilhelm Foundation, about teaching German education and art in Glasgow, ran to a meeting every couple of months with Hermann Muthesius up from the London embassy. She would range all over the life of the Clyde: the broadest definition of 'the major arts of life'. But how would this show up, and in whose dossiers?

Always, Bob Cormack, who wrote for *Forward*, would say, when you began to despair, something would happen: a signwriter or tram-conductor would start quoting Browning or playing Schumann on an ancient upright, and then for a few minutes the place would magically reformulate itself around the eternal. Even if it dissolved again, into cheap cigarettes and clothes which soon lost their shape, ideals battered and frustrated.

She and Bob had gone some distance ahead of the others, and for once he had stopped talking in his opinionated, ever-interesting, joke-cracking way. The tragic word-child: mouse-brown hair already thinning, shy, hopeful smile. And facing exile, probably eternally, from him, she softened, put aside her guard.

'They sport with us, the glorious ones: on their couches, tossing our fates carelessly about?"'

'Goethe, *Paerzenlied.*'

'Got it in one, ducks.'

They met when they'd been thrown together at a Bach Choir rehearsal, on her rebound from a handsome, idealist Irishman, an ex-priest some said, who had made her miserable. They had spent half-a-year of Friday evenings at Scottish Orchestra concerts or Carl Rosa operas. As grand passion it was getting nowhere, but it had its moments: the Dutchman's galleon practically crashing into the stalls, the first time they (and Glasgow) heard Bruckner Seven, the marvellous scherzo with its hunters on a snowy morning, Brahms' near-deafening artillery in the Goethe setting. The quartet rehearsed again and again; Lamond heartbreaking in the last piano pieces.

Was there, he sometimes wondered, someone else somewhere? Enigmatic Helena, continuously interesting: a cat who walked by herself.

They reached the edge of the cliff, where the rocks plunged towards the Clyde in tangles of dwarf-oak. The long sunset light burnished the cornfield to the east, gilded the white-walled farm. Above the smoky breath of Glasgow showed a sliver of moon.

'When are you going back?'

'Next Thursday, refugee transport: Leith to Rotterdam. Then train to Stendal. That's near to Berlin. You ought to visit sometime. But not now.'

And suddenly there was a sad frown on that usually ironic face, and her lip trembled. He believed what she did. In Germany the Social Democrats seemed established, just waiting for the Kaiser to fall over. But in waiting they had grown complacent, or were really only interested in their jobs in the party structure. Against this, romantic Bob's embroideries, she called them: bits of Morris and Marx and Ruskin (mad), Carlyle (very mad):

'Liked it here, *trotz Alledem*?'

'For a' that. I wouldn't have known that, but for you.'

And suddenly she hugged him, quite unexpectedly, and let her head fall against his.

'There, I'm getting sentimental, but you have been . . . oh *liebenswuerdig* Bob!'

And she gave him a kiss, a real, moist, loving kiss, her tongue darting between his lips,

'There, across the thunder of the guns!' she said, and broke away.

Below them on a paddle steamer headed out to the islands, was raised the raucous voice of Glasgow saying goodbye to more than a working year. And further west, at the limit of their sight, the low white ghost of a steam yacht lay quiet in a bay.

'A dinna ken that boat, but yon's the *Juno*.'

Bob, who could switch dialect in mid-sentence, was back in his Doric, appropriately enough.

'We bike tae Largs, pit the bikes on the train. Doonhill a'the wey. But there is somethin' I do want to say to ye.'

He looked at her with that shy determination in his gentle, ugly face – get rid of that absurd moustache, Bob, for God's sake, she thought –

'Speak on.'

'I think you're observin' us. You're wan o' they *Parcae*, they Fates, a fell clever wumman.'

She had got the hang of the dialect which he easily and ably fell back into, as her own folk would do into Swabian or *Schwiezerduetsch*.

'You mind where I come frae, Motherwell? We went there on the bikes a month syne, an ye saw there's a big railway brig ower the Calder, cried Babylon Brig? Ah telt ye aboot it?'

She remembered vividly the dark, flaring town and more vaguely something about a fallen Utopia.

'It wis ca'd Babylon after Orbiston, one o' Robert Owen's schemes – him that ma feyther named me on – an' the young laird pit up the money for it, but his braw freens' were agin it, and the ministers an' muckle fermers, so they missca'd it Babylon an' it only lasted a couple o' year an fell apart.

'Yet the folk there werena' daft, and some went aff to Canada, an' some steyed put an' set up the Store, ye know, the Co-operative, an' that was before we'd got steel or proper steam engines or the electric. We could dae that for oorsels an' we could dae it noo, stead o' battleships. Imagine stead o' they rotten slums we built big towers like the Forth Bridge where folk can live above the smoke an' filth, an have wee touns on the flerrs, wi' gairdens an' pairks, an' windmills for the electric an' lifts. No daft, maybe possible, a twenty year on . . .'

They looked west, and the setting sun caught the smoke that scrolled from the paddler's red-and-black funnel, and they imagined the folk on the deck. Drunk with the setting sun. The landscape – where else was a land like this, the broad blue of the lower firth, its little towns with their spires and dormered cottages, rocky beaches writhing with seawrack, exotic plantations out of which protruded baronial tower, Italianate belvedere. Not least Portencross, Duncan Muir's castle.

August 1914: Berlin, Kriegsmarineamt

A fortnight later Helena was in Berlin, staying with her father's sister to the west of the city centre: a place almost kin to 'respaictable' Glasgow, so that she now imagined the Berlin bourgeoise enunciating like their Kelvinside sisters the construction that met her kitten 'You caint haive kets in flets!' She would have gone to Unter den Linden on the S-Bahn, but they sent a young Badensier Captain von Velden to Oellendorferstrasse to collect her in a grand car, and there was much stamping and presenting-of-arms when they got to the Ministry, and always the clatter of boots in the corridor – so unnecessary but typical – until they reached the Administrative State-Secretary's office.

'Surprise! Alex!

'Gruess dich, liebe Helena, we are so much in your debt.' Alex Birnbaum had become one of Ballin's deputies. She knew him well from the Kultusministerium, a merry, cynical economist in a nest of professorial deadbeats. Now he didn't joke, and came directly to his point. 'We in this Abteilung were late in getting into this business. Frankly we didn't think of it at all until three months ago. Then we realised through your reports just how influential your remote river could be: enough to damage us – perhaps even fatally.'

'Meaning that you had only then actually bothered to look at my letters?'

His fingers washed each other, almost frenziedly. 'We were

understaffed. Too much was happening.' He had a cold and looked at her through his pince-nez with big, brimming eyes. Jewish, she knew, like at least half of her own circle. And then winced at the memory of his glacial boss, every inch *Preussich*: Winfried, Freiherr von und zu Stumm: blond head impaled on a ramrod-like linen stock, thoughts only of status, promotion, hierarchy.

'Then it wasn't priority. Now . . .'

'Be warned. When the British want to change, they change so rapidly you would not believe. No hierarchies – of commissioned officers or C4 professors. No having to listen to some doctoral idiot who hasn't had an original thought in years. That's what I have known. Do I want to help you? Objectively yes. As a socialist I agree with Marx: delenda est Russland. Subjectively no.'

'Why?'

'Because by October 1914 we will already have lost.'

'How so?'

'Schlieffen expected our army to take Paris in six weeks. But your war of movement will end in a month, and in a war of attrition and diplomatic pressure Britain has the advantage. You said that yourself.'

'England's army is tiny. Remember Bismarck: "If the English army invades, I shall send a policeman to arrest it." If they recruit volunteers they will take over a year to train.'

'It won't be *England's* army. It's Scots and Welsh and Irish. And they're not tinpot little Erbprinzen but proper political groups whom Lloyd George – that's who you'll face! – has got on his side.' (She remembered an almost-too-close encounter with the Welsh charmer in an Edinburgh hotel.)

Bugles sounded outside, and the clatter of hooves. Alex went to the window. 'His Majesty, always on the go.' His Majesty's relentless horse skittered at the approach of a staff car.

'Oh God. Helena, I agree almost totally with your – our – analysis but we don't go to His Transparency out there with our hands up. Brits in pieces is what he wants and what, two months ago we nearly had that with Carson and his Ulster rebels buying our guns. Can you let me have a page and a half of typescript by tomorrow morning on how we can get back there?'

'The face-to-face stuff?'

'Not something we talk about in the reports.'

The next evening Helena met Kuno Liebeskind in a near-empty (so arguably secure) café in Hackescher Markt. What was to be a famous affair had yet to begin; the editor was then suspected of undermining the generally pro-war Socialists. Helena had yet to take on the aura – the delicious danger – of a socialist Scherezade.

'Muir? Robust, potent, promiscuous – like his countryman the poet Burns. Also a successful business man with many connections. Right? He seems very close to the Chancellor (Finance-Minister *over here*) Lloyd George. Nearly led the anti-war party, now whipping the war-horses on. Could go either way – on one side talking about new weaponry, maybe even new strategies. Look at that.'

She dealt out photographs like playing cards.

'What?'

'They call it a 'Machine Gun Destroyer': Army couldn't care less. The Navy, God help us, is playing around with it. The 'floating airfield'? Pipe dream likewise –but just wait till the pressure's on. We Germans tend to go back to Sedan. The British go back to their American brothers and their Civil War: a different box-of-tricks entirely. Ingenious and impossibly destructive.'

'Have you ever read *News from Nowhere*? By the English artist Morris. He has a civil war in which ten million die. Followed by our sort of Werkbund utopia . . . about now, when you think of it. Compare

H G Wells and his *War of the Worlds*. Where's he now? At Wellington House.'

A conspiratorial grin was possible. Suppose knockout-blow notions give way to technical confrontation? A technical brouhaha which would change the world for good and all? End all of this for a start.'

The two had reached the point where the Landwehr-Kanal joined the Spree. A hundred metres away reared the vast bulk of the Stadtschloss: a waltz tune came from a first floor window.

'*Here* our workers sang your Mr Burns, sixty-six years ago – *Trotz Alledem*! – and the Royal Guards shot back.'

21 October 1914, Sandhills House, Helensburgh

Randolph Road, Helensburgh, was a solid, uninspired product of Clydeside Art Nouveau, three-storey houses, fairly new, surrounded by raw gardens whose monkey-puzzle trees successfully competed for the visitor's attention. It looked out over other smaller houses' gardens to the Clyde and on its southern bank to the sugarworks of Greenock and their chimneys. From time to time, when the wind was south-easterly, their rather sickly smell and the rattle of riveting from Scott's shipyard was borne across. This didn't happen too often, which was why Randolph Road remained pricey and select.

Sandhills House was the property of Adam Halley, but on this morning, 21 October 1914, his life fell apart. A car called with two detectives at 11 am. He was arrested, handcuffed to one of the detectives and driven to Dumbarton Police Station. There he was charged with treason by a magistrate, remanded in custody, taken down to the cells, divested of documents and valuables, stripped naked, washed, issued with prison clothing, and put into a solitary cell.

Halley had had a couple of hours' prevision of what was going to happen to him; it did little either to prepare or console. John Clyde, Mackay & Company's KC, phoned up. The message was terse and unpromising, 'Lord Advocate Munro is a strong party Liberal, and is out to jail Jack Bonar, head of MacKays. We think we may have got him off, but it will be at the expense of others in the firm.'

That meant him and Sinclair Lee, the other executive concerned with day-to-day running. They had signed off the transactions in question. These were sent off each week in a package to Jack Bonar who had theoretically the right of veto, but had never in years exercised it. Clyde's legal line was that this procedure was determined by the duty executives.

'We will do what we can.' was all Halley could get.

After what he had been through in the last month! Since that first telegram that the SS *Themis* had sailed from Sydney, Nova Scotia. Her cargo of 7000 tons of iron ore was already the property of RheinStahl, Duisburg, so she was serving the enemy. But that was how the iron business was carried out. Revoke the agreement and Mackay and Company, their Glasgow firm with long German links, could be down by £ 50,000. Sinclair Lee had rung Bonar, who suggested two things. One: try to halt the ship in the Channel (she had no radio); two: renegotiate the contract in Rotterdam.

Halley found himself on Dungeness beach. Wireless cables to transatlantic liners yielded sightings of the Norwegian tramp. If they plotted speed, weather, etc., right she should turn up in three days' time; and inbound craft usually picked up signals from the flag station. Two-three days. No sign and thick mist. 'Cable Rotterdam.' came from Glasgow. Done, but word was the *Themis* was already in port; the cargo had been transferred to barges. The Rotterdam manager Vanderwyck had cabled Bonar, and – accepting silence as consent – the shipment went ahead.

But there were intercepts, Mackay's bankers were suborned. Bonar was warned, the two subordinates arrested. Some weeks later, over lunch at the Western Club, Dr Osborne Mavor reported to Muir on a chat with Clyde.

'Tory boss Law – and Munitions-Director Weir – want Clyde to be

Lord Advocate. Thinks Munro's incompetent. He wants a hard line on the actual Clyde.'

'How best to do that?'

'Make Munro Scottish Secretary, carry him clean oot o' the legal side.'

'How?'

'Give him a scalp, preferably a small one.'

Within a fortnight a court date was set, the trial carried out, pleas of mitigation considered – to some extent – and the two accused returned to prison for a further five months solitary confinement. But the Glasgow legal establishment had done its discreet work. Little publicity had been made of the case, and the fact that one of Glasgow's leading merchant houses had been supplying Krupps with its iron ore was left for Irish malcontents to raise. With Clyde now at his Edinburgh desk in Parliament House; Weir, Munitions Controller, Scotland, with Muir as factotum, had the river to themselves.

May 1915: The New Minister

'We stretch to sandwiches here, and not much more.' The big Whitehall room was pitifully bare. A couple of armchairs, a long trestle table, two telephones, drifts of files

And in the middle of it, the Minister of Munitions David Lloyd George.

'Jesus Christ our Lord was fundamentally sound. Avoid going above twelve. Under it, you can usually agree on who to trust and do the consultation down the phone.'

Then, almost off-hand:

'Dr Muir, Dr Addison – a real Doctor like the immortal Watson, a sawbones who has run a teaching hospital – while you and I are conjurors who call ourselves statesmen or captains of industry or doctors of philosophy or law, etc.'

Lloyd George and his Watson had, however, done their work. The questions came logically. The manner was alternately as energetic as a wind-up toy, barking at underlings, jumping to the ring of telephones;

then friendly, almost conspiratorial, like being initiated into a schoolboy gang.

'First, can I call you Duncan? Not familiarity, but I'm Welsh so calling people by surnames is pointless. Coffee, coffee.'

He gesticulated at a girl who smiled and darted away.

'I've ten minutes to convince you.'

He threw himself into the armchair, shot his cuffs forward, clasped his hands.

'I know your Fabian stuff. Useful people, used them a lot in Trade. They tell me: good employer, thinks strategically – damn few in this country do – cutting-edge stuff. Know the Germans well. We have to, if we're going to take them on.'

How was Muir to force himself into this torrent? Every time he tried, some new inspiration hit that alarmingly white head.

'Minister, we've overcapacity, which is important.'

'And from what Willie Weir and Haldane tell me, you know how to use it. Sorry, I'll shut up in a moment. But let me tell you where I find myself: somewhere totally new. War in our age is like a huge industry, organised in departmental detail and rarin' to go. But in peacetime it isn't joined up. Given war, individual bits must be brought together, planned in series, set against dates. Then the right horsepower takes over – and it'll transform it. Like the railway before and after the Stephensons. Now you.'

Muir glanced past him momentarily, and noted that one of the piles of volumes on the floor was a set of *The Children's Encyclopaedia*. He explained about his sessions in Hamburg with the Bergius engineering board. The quality of their technology, the menace they could become if they really got ahead . . .

'But they are Germans. There's a point where someone rides into the lab on a horse.'

'As I thought. Well, he'll be as dense as our own lot. A tiny army can be a great advantage.'

'My view is that we can match them. They have no idea of the dimensions of what they're taking on, and how things like lorries and planes will affect the mix. Internal combustion is the great unknown. If we can get in early, and buy up the stuff we need on the international market, if necessary from . . . er, ah, um . . . Switzerland . . . and pile a lot into research and development, especially with the radio-and-plane combination to hand . . .'

Westermain would have been gratified, but he stayed unmentioned. There had been some friction between the pair, hinted at by propagandist Masterman.

'Weir takes that line too. Bundle of energy, but a bit Prussian too. But that's where you will be.

The minister turned to his other assistant,

'TeeJay – Apologies for this!'

He talked rapidly and unintelligibly. The reply, likewise, was in Welsh. The twinkly glance seemed to say 'One up on you.'

'Our national secret weapon.'

Muir had heard of this. 'Every human quality except trust.'

'You know about diesels. Also, you're on good terms with Labour'.

Muir nodded.

'Wouldn't have known a diesel from a petrol engine six weeks ago. I damn well do now. Petrol's planes and cars, diesel's lorries and submarines and . . . well . . . caterpillar tractors. If we get that one wrong, they'll scrag us.'

Whitehall-Soho, 'In the Patriarch's Days'

'You had better, I suppose, get used to this.'

They had quit Whitehall and were walking briskly in the direction of Soho.

'Lady Emily here?'

'No. In South America. But do you know a Mrs Aitchison, also from Glasgow?'

'Sister of Constance Reid. Who's on my staff.'

'She's in London and bewildered. Shall we have her along?'

'Can you ring her?'

Muir nodded. Cathy was at the Grand Babylon.

'That's good. Ring her from Bertorelli's and tell her to take a taxi. My assistant Miss Stevenson gets so browned-off with business talk – and poor Puss, she's had enough of that for a month – that she'll want someone to relax with.'

Cathy arrived and – which hadn't always been the case in the past – took instantly to her new friend.

'I take it,' said Lloyd George, 'that we all know what's up and this isn't going to cause any of us to run screaming out of the place, so I would suggest a litre of the Chianti. Cathy, you are au fait with Doctor Muir's professional career and high-maintenance boss? Occasional shop-talk won't disturb you?'

There was pasta and herbs and olive oil and garlic, followed by veal escalopes, fritate and runny cheese.

'Not much chance of being ambushed by party Liberals unless they're on the ran-dan and we therefore have something on them. Besides they all have positively dreadful cooks whom they pay to poison them. Except Haldane.'

'Always except Haldane.'

'You know him?' Lloyd George turned to the girls, 'Tory idiots turfed him out. Ten years older than me. Once upon a time was engaged to Ronnie Munro-Ferguson's sister but she gave him the heave. Then he decided that Hegel and haute cuisine were better bets.'

'I knew his sister, friend of Edward Caird. Something of a socialist,'

'So's Haldane, but a rather grand one. Our link to the Fabians and Bernard Shaw.'

And there they were, a middle-aged man and Muir, a relative youth, discussing with two fairly young but liberated women an unorthodox lifestyle in a fortunately nearly-totally-uncomprehending environment.

'Men of the left – you'd still claim that, Duncan, wouldn't you? – in the crazy position of running this astonishing war because the prospect of handing munitions over to the military leaves us distraught.'

'So you want us as the maiden tribute?' from Frances,

'Bits of fluff with a degree?' added Cathy.

'Watch it, Miss Stevenson, Mrs Aitchison. Or I will swap you for H G Wells's latest.'

'Sauce!'

'But isn't it extraordinary? Here we are, in a bohemian alien restaurant in London, rearming Britain: something we're almost in our guts opposed to, but we think we can do better than the generals.'

'Our paid killers.'

'With their wives at court or in dull Camberley villas, their daft ideas about everything outside the forces.'

'And even dafter ideas about everything within.'

'Do you know Umberto Wolff?' asked the minister.

'No.'

'Nice, vaguely Italian. Introduced me to this place. Defined our officer class as "strong, silent and barking mad".'

'Who am I to disagree?'

'What you've done, Duncan, is show me the Clyde's potential. You're a professional, but you seem to have insight: that aircraft carrier scheme, they tell me, might work. No-one else could have done it, not even Tom Jones here, late of Glasgow Uni, who put me on to you. We needed someone who could get round – sorry – get on with Labour, and it might work. And you have the benefit of Cathy here, for my poor neglected Puss.'

And he looked at Frances in the way one of Wells's clerks would have regarded a well-set milliner in Croydon. It had form. Duncan remembered how at eleven he had met Gladstone and his Catherine at Dalmeny – both near ninety – and was almost shocked at their revelry in risqué Music Hall. While Frances had the air of a girl at the seaside, glorying in her Young Man. It was transparently sincere, which made it touching in a way that his delicacies in the matter of Mrs Aitchison – on both sides, it had to be said – were not.

May 1915 Carlisle: MacGillivray unpacks

Cathy Aitchison skirted a man in a brown frieze coat on the Carlisle platform: slicked-down grey hair, hatchet face, gold specs, vaguely familiar. Muir thought he might be an Ulsterman called MacGillivray, encountered during the 1912 Home Rule stramash. An MI5 regular he thought. Why here?

Avoid eye contact? Not a chance.

'Doctor Muir, I believe. Will Yr'Honour spare me a seat?'

Seconds later hatchet-face was in the compartment, rattled out identification in Ulster English. He put down a bag on the table and removed a file.

'Masterman telegraphed and I picked it up at Stranraer. I'm on my way to report on Gretna and thought I'd better nab you. We have twenty minutes'

The documents had been photographed and highlighted. Two were unpleasant. 'Ye've heard of Hannay's coup agin the Black Stone gang. That's the boss Appleby after he was hangit. No nice. The Jerries got haud o't an pit him oot as a Polish priest lynched by the Russkies. Smart footwork. That's where we are.'

The rest of his discourse went further into gobbledygook. The New Army was sucking in skilled men and turning them into amateur infantry, which would take eighteen months. Meanwhile thousands of civvies – women, Irish – were transforming shipyards and engineering-shops into shell and gun factories. In the background was, episodically, an Irish-German-American plot. Could he help get an agent to US? Capitalise on the Mackay business and get Adam Halley out of prison and Scotland and working on it over there? Could he oblige?

30 May 1915: Watson Wilson at the Midland, Manchester

'Mr Wilson?'

'Call me Watson, or if ye ken me better, Wattie. Myra, this is Dr Muir.'

The girl smiled sweetly. She was petite with her dark red hair in a page-boy. Carrying off a shot-silk dress of turquoise, with cream lace at the throat and cuffs. Pretty calves, with a hint of muscle: a classy hoofer, Muir guessed. Happy to be with Watson, her present beau, but seemingly quite independent. Watson was in a business suit of blue-grey worsted, a northern *commercant*, like the others in the Grand Salon, apart from the accent.

'Miss Gemill?'

'Myra'll dae. We're on at seven at the Empire, other end o' Oxford Street. Myra's got shoppin' tae dae. Tap-dancin' shoes.'

'We go through them like hankies. We've a ragtime number with Mr Fred, who dances us off our feet. Have you heard of him, Mr Muir? He's quite homely, as the Americans say – "Can't act, can't sing, can dance a little." See him dance and he's pure joy.'

The girl's face lit up in a way quite different from the stylised obliqueness of the Ministry girls. As she left, her body swayed delicately in a way that delighted both men.

Muir unpacked the gadget. It wasn't unfamiliar to Wilson, though he had never used one.

'You just speak into this tube, and the machine takes it down on the wax roll. It's what we call a recorder. One of my girls with touch-typing will transcribe from it. Then we melt and reuse it.'

'Whit d'ye want me to say?'

'You could tell us how you got into this business. It'll act as a sort of introduction.'

'How far d'ye want me tae gang back – sorry, to go back –

'Talk as you would normally, this time round. But in standard English for the reports.'

'How did that happen?' and Muir clicked the switch . . .

'Well, at fifteen I was whit they ca' an upstanding youth, an apprentice chef at the Central Hotel, and getting interested in the girls and, in a mild way, in the Independent Labour Party. That or football, an' no way was I going to stand in Saturday rain bein' showered wi' bigots. Then I got something called Krohn's syndrome. Never been properly researched, but it hits your lower gut. I was in the infirmary for a sixmonth, an' was lucky to get oot. The surgeons fiddled aboot down there, pu'ed me back frae the grave, but at the end o't I was told I couldnae faither bairns. It was then I started to organise my memory, an' more than that.

'Nurses are good people but they arena' saints. Hoo can ye be when life's a' bedpans and blood? In fact they're pretty direct aboot it. So one o' them saw first hand that I was well provided for, so to say, an' we got to know each other as I recovered. Marie was Irish. She wasna' the marrying kind, nor shy. I got invited to her flat in Anniesland, told my stories, cooked her a meal. An' afterwards there we are on the sofa, an' she pits her hand there an' says 'Gosh!' an' cannae get oot o her corset fast enough. I was aa ower the place tae begin with, then I got the hang o it. "Like riding a bicycle" she said. I got aa my social education yon nicht.

'I was relieved Marie wasna' the sort o lass that clung to ye and, good for her, put the word aroon her friends. I've no lacked for company then, nor since. An I went on the halls wi' my Memory Man act, startin' in parts o' the coalfield an after a couple o' years getting the length of the Empire. You know, 'If they like you, they let you live!'

'A wee, wan chiel, stick-thin. Lookit as if the wind wad blaw him ower. Lives on breid an' saps, cause o' his bowels, puir soul. But by Goad, he can talk to trade. If wars could be won by stories, he wis Alexander the

Great. Lord Haldane taks' me to him, in a fell grand hoose off Whitehall afore a big bleezing fire. There he is in a captain's uniform that doesna' suit him, hings on him like a tent, pile o' cables in one hand, smoking a fag like a squaddie. He fetches twae packets an' gies me one.

'Aye Wattie', he says, nae mair the grand laird, but more an easy-going fermer or kirk elder. 'They say I write too much about grand folk in big London clubs. Which this is an' so I do. But ye, the son o' a postie, beat them a'. It's no just your memory that attracts a' yir women – that's as much as we'll blether aboot them, tho' sometimes I wish I had yir gift. But ye're a fortunate man.

'Let's tae business. Ye say ye cannae forget anything, an' ye seem able tae arrange it somewhere in yir heid so ye can get back tae it. Ah'm no that bad masel, but no on that level; but ye get aboot the place. Ye talk to folk, forbye yir lady friends. An' ye can spout it a' like a gramophone. If ye can mak' siller oot o yir brain: be Mister Memory, we need you, an' you're made.'

'So there I am in an' amang the great. 'Sir William Weir, Mr Watson Wilson. Sir William, tell this young man aboot yir new self-acting turret lathe, whit its size is, whit it can do – an a' that. Better still, show him the plans.'

And Sir Wullie, a wee keelie like me, only rich, does his stuff. I do mine, an' then he's properly amazed.

The thing is, of course, if someone shows me anything: a newspaper, a blueprint, I can remember it in a general way. If they tell me to scan it, I can do that. Ah hiv tae be telt whit to look for but, that said, I'm a camera.

'What John and Wullie did – that's what we ca'd each ither – wis tae put me on a circuit like roon' the Ha's. Or rather no' roon the Ha's but "entertaining the war workers" as they pit it: Woolwich, Sheffield,

Manchester, Glasgow, Woolwich. Collect the facts, keep them in yir heid, get a notion of whit 'morale' wis like, then record it. I get to stay in wan o' the big railway hotels, talk to the intelligence boys in the forenoon, hang aboot the factory in the efternoon an' when the show ends the hotel staff will wink at me gien' a nice wee girl from the chorus a guid feed in a grand private room, wi' a' the trimmings and a bath fit for Cleopatra.

'Why did they dae' it? No' the girls, but Buchan an' Co? Weel, they were feart o' Jerry spies. They thought that the place was fair hoachin' wi' waiters semaphorin' at Zeppelins frae the rooftops. They were clever laddies frae Oxford, an' thocht the Jerries were as gleg. As ye ken, Mr Muir, from your time in Hamburg, they were no. But they were feart themsel, an ither folk peyed them to fricht them. Result: thirty-thoosand frae Godnosewhere in one works alane, yon big one at Gretna makin' cordite. As he says "Ye're a lang wey frae bein' an idiot, Wattie, an' mair useful than dozens in red tabs an' polished boots.'

Muir couldn't get a berth on the overnight sleeper so moped in a reserved first-class. Moped over Intelligence and whatever MacGilveray had been up to. Moped over that 30,000 Irish on munitions work, only partly reassured by the remarkable Watson Wilson and his reports. Moped over whatever in the Great Scheme of Things he was supposed to be doing: was he a technical organiser or a superior spy?

June 1915: death from the sea
Muir would remember until he died every detail of one night a month later. He detrained at Euston, taxi'd to the Whitehall office to pick up correspondence, then walked to his hotel along the Embankment. Male London, ulstered and umbrella'd against a freakish easterly, slouched towards Charing Cross and electric trains. No further from here than

Manchester their brothers and sons and uncles were soaking in trenches, crawling on idiotic sorties through barbed wire to kill or be killed by an equally alienated enemy. Thousands of miles away border lads were baking on the Bosphorous, over against Troy, making no headway against an old ally, now an enemy, trying to aid a Russian steamroller failing to fire up. In months his great new guns would send shells whining into the night, arcing over the shattered battlefields, little villages converted to churned-up mud – to smack into concrete and make more mud, red this time.

At the centre of this mad machine was Wattie the mnemonic boy, this Dionysius with his cast of lovely, adoring women. Like the man he'd heard about on the *Titanic*, who was so drunk the firewater in his bloodstream kept him alive, while the innocent, sober survivors froze to death and went under. Or, and he paused for a moment, remembering the Banqueting Hall, one of those Rubens satyrs sporting with nymphs in clouds high above the blood and agony of the battlefields on which royal authority depended.

At the other end there was poor Rupert Brooke – 'thoughts of high laughter, loveliness and ease' – known in Cambridge along with Hugh Dalton, through the Fabians, who had somehow caught the idealist spirit in August 1914. A decent fighter with the Marines at Antwerp. Idealism had barely survived his death from blood-poisoning on that Aegean island. And himself – pacifistic, semi-American, almost-German. Midwife to this frightening new world, bad now, likely to be much worse.

Much worse arrived promptly. At the Club's desk there was a cable from the Munitions Directorate: the P & O liner *Carinthic* had been sunk by torpedo off the Lizard. Emily and Robbie Rattray, returning from South America, were passengers. In the morning another cable 'Reach Paddington two-thirty. Emily gone. RR.'

Sir Robbie turned up, alone and desolate.

'The boat had remoonts frae Argentina, forbye a host o' bairns, maistly o' grooms an' gauchos. Emly kent aboot the horses, which are legally "munitions", and wis beside hersel aboot the bloody eedjits whae'd authorised it. She got the bairns – or as many of them as she could – awa. Then as she was makin' for the last boat, she found wan wee bunch that were stuck, so she steyed on wi' them.'

She had been, in her great travelling cloak, like a furious mother hen with her chicks, on that sloping deck. The ship had suddenly canted over as he had tried to reach them, and Sir Robbie had been thrust into the sea. He tried to bear up, but was choked with grief, which burst from him in gouts of tears – 'Ah'm sorry, Muir, but she was aa' ah ever had . . .'

Muir held him, almost like a lover,

'Cry, man, for God's sake.'

Apart from the early blaze of sexual passion, the Muirs hadn't been emotionally well-matched, though they worked well within the little republic of the Dumbarton yard, realising mutually that Emily, like Lord Curzon's India, functioned best as 'an independent and not always friendly power'. Sir Robbie was the best thing that could have happened to her. Now bereft, he had one wife mad and one lover dead, and was inconsolable.

But Muir was also practical, and Robbie an industrial-strength slaughterer? No. Not a good or wise description . . . better 'industrial victualler'? QED on a grand scale. Armies marched on their stomachs. Muir drafted a cable to the boss.

3

Daedalus

*'Heard the heavens fill with shouting,
and there rain'd a ghastly dew
From the nations' airy navies grappling
in the central blue.'*

June 15: 'No other Troy'

Another meeting-room, another film. Busy shots of battleships, transports, encampments couldn't disguise the fact that the eastern strategy was stuck. Muir was there wearing his Lieutenant-Commander (Naval Reserve) gear, supposedly to reassure, but conscious that he knew more about the mess than the generals and admirals present.

The Dardanelles expedition – to force a 'warm-water' link to Russia via the Black Sea – looked good in the abstract. But twenty men from Selkirk, close to Alderbank House, had vanished in a single day. Missing presumed dead. On a peninsula opposite Troy, but without Achilles or Agamemnon, Turkey, old ally, now the least-regarded of the King's enemies, could be taken on by a second-division force of obsolescent ships. In theory. Instead its mines and torpedos had sunk them. Steamers trying to offload troops became sitting ducks. Breakouts were futile. Cheery Tommies, Aussies, Kiwis went down to malaria. Daft assaults on the locals piled up the losses: the Turks didn't take prisoners. Obvious that combined operations involving eighty-thousand odd demanded new communications, air cover, radio, totally new sorts of ship.

Muir didn't play the Westermain-Robertson scheme but outlined the need for full-utility support-ships. This was 'amateur stuff, self-advertisment' to the senior Admiral present. The audience clucked their agreement, but someone, Welsh, from the Exchequer, took his card . . .

June 1915: North British Hotel, Glasgow, a Solitary

Watson Wilson, now 'Mr Memory' of the Halls, and Muir were drinking a consolatory evening whisky in the grand tiled bar of the North British. Around them Arkwright, Dalton, Whitworth, in stained-glass and tile, were getting on with the Industrial Revolution. Two important people were due at eight prompt. One was an AFC pilot called Lauchland, the other was Westermain's protégé Ernest Robertson.

'A solitary, ye could ca' him. Someone whae's heid rins on strange, partic'liar tracks. If ye needit tae draw a' the muscles and banes o' the thing thegither, he'd dae it for ye. It takes yin tae ken yin, an' ye ken me, Doctor Muir.

'Duncan, from now on.'

'Very well . . . he stertit as mechanic in a jute-mill in Dundee, then got in wi' a faimly ca'd Murray wha went in for airplanes, gliders ye ken. He read up in a' the buiks and could, efter he'd gang'd tae the Tech, tak a' they engines tae bits, as if he wis a surgeon. Duncan, ye could dae worse.'

'That was what you used to get in the old Scottish families – like mine.' said Muir, who had got his pipe going. 'Great clans of folk from all over the West, meeting once a New Year in somebody's big hoose, everyone from grand uncles in Parliament to auld bodies from cottages in the backlands. The thing was that they kept their lads o' pairts, often damn awkward folk, alive and got them scholarships, covered up when some of their schemes were plain crazed. People like Adam Smith and

Samuel Smiles said that it was from our douce Calvinist burghers that progress came, following their simple economic ideas. To my mind it was much more inspired, much dafter: more like Smith himself in fact. A genius who couldnae' tie his ain shoelaces.'

Muir became expansive, 'We Scots believed then in common sense, which isn't just being practical. In fact, it's half-way to the mystical. What it meant then was a sort of power that mediated between all the other areas of sense-perception: touch, taste, sight, smell, hearing, and codified your responses. Was it a soul? At any rate it kept the theologians busy. Or was it a kink in the brain that wired up some sections together, enabling connections, but not others? Strangely, we've never attempted to understand it clinically. We don't know how many of these people there are. They don't know themselves – are there a couple of hundred, or thousands? Do they work better as individuals or in groups? Are these gifts linked to culture – like music? Is it what fascinates us about these Russians, their ability to co-ordinate themselves, to endure, to dance. Do we fail because we're 'das Land ohne Musik?'

'Aboot that, I'm no' qualified to judge. Captain Buchan cannae sing a note. Ye can but observe oor Mr Robertson. There's naethin o' him that's logical, except that he gangs at his ain schemes right tae the end, forbye no' being a' that great at pittin' then ower. Yet they're a' weighed and written, an' the sums gang right. Committees o' admirals couldnae' get further. Noo we've got the wireless, an' the planes tae carry it, an' send it to the ships – but whit for, except that they're no damn' guid? Oor siller's gaed in the wrang place. Robertson's schemes may be daft, but if they worked, his planes could sink maist o' Germany's U-Boats.'

Under the surface of this *plauderie* was a big idea. When Muir hit it he felt a jolt like an electric shock: as if he were driving very fast on the wrong side of a road. Watson was right. The Munitions programme – Lloyd George – would give the generals what they said they wanted, but they too were tyros. Lloyd George's war machine demanded a root-and-branch reorientation: but its success had actually strengthened the country's most conservative element: so self-absorbed that a music hall turn had to point this out.

'Duncan! D'ye hear me?' He came to.

'Only too well.'

'Anyhow, Duncan, when thae lads turn up, whit do we dae?'

'You have your bags?'

'Upstairs an' packed.'

'Then, as the auld dominie said, we dae whit we're telt!'

Minutes later two figures materialised in the entrance. One was tall in a brown belted tweed coat, the other short, shy and white-haired. The tall man summoned them.

'We've a reserved compartment on the 8.30 to Ardrossan, and sail first thing tomorrow. Be on Platform Seven at St Enoch's in twenty minutes.'

June 1915: Machrihanish, de Bridoon's war

Muir and William Weir, Clyde Munitions Controller, PO Lauchland and Robertson took the morning steamer across a slatey sea to dull Campbeltown, and a small, elegant train puffed across the peninsula to Machrihanish, where, well beyond the western straits, the Atlantic raved. The golf-course fairway was generous, and where it wasn't the bunkers had been flattened for the experimental planes. In the wind-thrashed Clubhouse the Commandant, an ex-cavalry Major called Hubert de Bridoon sprawled himself over the sofa, a figure of some presence, exceeding even the cavalry's ration of well-bred nonchalance. Muir remembered someone in the Naval Reserve claiming to have seen Hubie in his prime in dialogue with Lord Roberts, the old Commander in Chief:

'What, Mr de Bridoon, do you conceive as the use of cavalry in modern war?'

'Why, to give tone to what would oth'wise be a mere vulgah bwawl.'

Muir surmised that de Bridoon, horseless, was like a lobster in the

Sahara, but he had found a sort of niche fretting over his collection of flying contraptions. He would annex bits of it from time to time to venture 'over there' to Bridoonstown where he couldn't have been any crazier than his relatives.

He allowed them to take a two-seater Sopwith Seapup up and fly to Stranraer. A submarine had been sent out earlier that day with instructions to sail on the surface, submerge on battery drive at periscope level, dive to deep submerge, and they were given rough co-ordinates about where it would be. Westermain, now gazetted lieutenant, was allocated to him as pilot: somehow now become both more than human, and encased in a memorably dirty, grease-smeared uniform. The plot was to recognise and describe the surface trails. Hubie would be escorting in a single seater.

Hubie's introduction hadn't been fulsome to either Westermain or Robertson, his other charge: 'Vewwy stwange. In his own little wold. Inside it, quite fawmidable. Outside – have you evah seen a naked tawtise?'

Muir hadn't.

'Not pweasant. And Westermain bawely makes sense most of the time. No social gwace. But he has ideahs about – aecwaeft cawwiahs it sounded like – which might just wok.'

Then with firmness:

'We need to know whey big bad Boche keeps his subs.' Said de B

'In big bad Belgium. In Flanders where they don't much care for the French.'

'Thought so. How do we gawner intelligence?' He went on

'Base our people in Holland where it's easy enough to slip over the frontier. They can calculate the length of sorties, time spent recuperating in port. If we get timings, know where they'll get to and at what time, we can be waiting for 'em. Better still, hit 'em just outside their bases, so they block the channels.'

'Way-ull', says de B, 'youah man Westermain – isn't he on the plane with them? – alweady thea.' With his cawwiahs. Y'kno, he's built one, Blackness Castle.'

'The beach?'

'It can be done.'

Muir recollected Hubie's frenzied attack on the bookshelves to find the tide tables.

'Aha! Between ten and twelve suicidal, then at least tomowwow alwight fo' five hows. Dwy as a bone. Fancy a twip, Muah?'

Twelve hours later, the morning having – with the sun – turned from louring to glittery, they were airborne: flying *Alauda Magna* into the wind at sixty miles an hour. Below them a black-funnelled Donaldson liner, outward-bound, trailed smoke. Some coasters off Larne, and a tiny train taking Derry passengers from the Stranraer boat. In Lough Swilly the substantial corpse of the split-new dreadnought *Audacious* which had hit a mine and sunk.

Hubie gesticulated with his right hand.

'Theah she blows.' Came down the speaking tube.

And there was the submarine, slowly surfacing from periscope depth but still nakedly visible. Muir could see why. From a surface ship its hull would be difficult to make out from the waves; now its grey pencil stood out against the water, the rocks, the weed-patches. Figures poured from its conning tower and manned its quickfiring gun. Hubie waggled his wings at the men on deck and the sub's machine gun emitted little puffs of smoke – firing blanks – then he banked left, looped and came back more slowly on the same course. Further puffs of smoke.

A live bullet whacked into *Alauda Magna*'s wing.

'Told 'em to do that.' Said Hubie in the Bridoonstown saloon an hour later.

'You complete lunatic!'

'Vewwy unusual faw 'em to get wange, let alone elevation, deah boy. Point to pwoove is that we could get in thea with time to dwop a towpeedo, and yah-boo to thea ickle popgun.'

'I don't bloody care. Damn nearly blew us to bits.'

'Yeth you do cae, Muah, cos I've just made youa point faw you. Ain't it so, Bessie?'

And the spinster of his two sisters at the Big House said grimly, 'Probably at the cost of your job, Hubert,' then turned more kindly to Muir. 'We'll be so upset if you can't stay for dinner, Dr Muir.'

He could see the other sister, Nessie, scrambling across the yard after a brown hen, murder in every leap.

'Do you play whist? We haven't managed a four in weeks.'

Outside, the Errigal range rose across the lough, purple and green, with flecks and folds of gold where the sun burst through the cloud, and on the strand the yellow of their firm – but very temporary – aerodrome.

'Ah, the bwuvva-in-law!' A dark-featured, keen-looking man strode into the room.

'You must be Muir. Welcome to the seventeenth century.'

Two freckled energetic boys and as many dogs capered at his legs. 'Don't mighty decisions depend on sheer chance?'

'If we braise it with leeks and carrots and sherry we'll have something that'll power ye back to Glasgow. *Sotto voce: Larry, who **is** he?* Now clear off with the boys and Mr Muir to the headland and work up an appetite in him.'

'I've had a look at your engine and can do something with it. But back to chance. Hubie got Machrihanish set up because I was here; I fly and know about engines, while he can use the little Campbeltown railway works for metal-bashing. And otherwise keep out of the way of the boys on the Clyde. Though it's all against the odds, your thing might just work on this crazy schedule.'

'Hasn't intwoduced himself, wude boy.'

He perched himself on the kitchen table as Nessie bustled in with the dead chicken and an armful of ingredients, aimed at the great range.

'Out! out! Or else no supper.'

The plain white house in its wind-bent grove dwindled behind them.

'Larry Doyle, civil engineer. Broadbent and Doyle, Baker Street and Rosscullen. Heard of? Lord BroadBee, an exalted bit of your ministry, tipped me off. I think this war's rubbish, but your lot makes so many mistakes – he jabbed an arm in Hubie's direction – I have to be here to save life.'

They walked out with the evening swimming in, the freckled boys and their dogs gallivanting along the track to Mizen Head. The wind had dropped and the clouds were massing to the west.

'The might of the mighty Atlantic', yelled Larry as they breasted the path and saw the ocean hurl itself at the pillars and tunnels of the cliff. 'The sheer power, the millions of tons of water in motion. Sooner or later we'll master it, and won't have to fight each other in the dark for coalfields or slaves.'

'We're a deceptive lot, Muir. 'Catholic', for a start. The de Bridoons look a self-caricature, and brother Hubie could win prizes at it, but in practical terms we're materialist atheists. Only not very efficient at it.

'The problem about people like your Robertson and Hubie is that they're far dafter than even this war, but the circumstances give them their chance. Robertson's right about planes and ships. A plane is a flying gun: a machine-gun for killing other planes, a torpedo for killing anything that floats. Short flying time, short-range, but add radio, proper carriers, catapults, flying decks, faster, heavier planes: a years' work and you could sink the Ostend U-boats and the High Seas Fleet. Because everything's short-term, economics goes out the window. Hubie would have waved his sabre and charged the guns at Balaclava but he, Westermain and Robertson are on to something huge. And afterwards?'

'Perpetual peace?'

'Dream on, friend.'

June 1915: 'Whuppity Stourie' on the Road to Troon

Two days later, after visiting Cathy Aitchison (her housekeeper was away on a shopping morning and he fared remarkably well) Muir, spruce and tomcat-sharp in the bright, spring sun, found himself being chased down a suburban street in Cathcart by a small, smart yellow Argyll car steered by a tweed-clad figure in a check motoring coat.

'I say, Muir, where you off to?'

It was Osborne Mavor, well known to Muir, mentioned in the context of scientific effervescence by Westermain on that journey to Preston, which now seemed to have occurred years before.

'Troon.'

'Want a lift? Wild horses would not keep me or Whuppity Stoorie, which I'm driving, from the burgh of Troon on such a day as this.'

Muir swung himself up and on to the high passenger-seat. Mavor bestowed a sunny glance on him:

'Some of us, Scots in particular, have personalities so huge we have to build lean-tos to accommodate them. Like my friend Bridie.'

'Bridie?'

'Our tasty if not particularly healthy Scots confection of sausage-meat and onions, done up in pastry. Of the people, like haggis. But there's nothing elevated or harmonious about "Mr Haggis".'

'So?'

'I employ Mr Bridie to mock the Scots, as my friend Bernard Shaw mocks the English. They need this salutary discipline, otherwise they verge on an excess of self-confidence, qualifying as smugness.'

Mavor smiled with his own brimming confidence, twinkling his large spectacled eyes at an obliging world.

'Avanti! Forward to Troon!'

They indeed ran forward, the morning sun sending the car's shadow flying west along the tranquil Paisley Road. Periodically they would pass a tramcar gliding along, or meet another automobile, right to right, otherwise only slow horse carts of various sorts, delivering sacks, bottles and tins to small dusty shops. They cantered at 40 mph past several varieties of church, ducked under and rattled over freight railway lines where pug engines butted clinking wagons into mine or foundry. Villas gave way to tangled, weedy, neglected fields, marked down for building; clutches of miners' rows, smoky and smelly; the occasional gatehouse of a big estate.

Accustomed to make that journey on the South-Western railway, Muir appreciated the new view, and the sight of a green engine and its carriages overtaking him on his right. Yet he could neither talk to Dr Mavor nor, as he usually did, write or read the newspaper. He found that vaguely irritating. Mavor apparently didn't.

At Kilwinning they breasted a hill and surveyed the Clyde: choppy, grey-flecked with cloud, rain over Arran. There was a clump of birch trees by the road, masking the white cottage of a small farm, a stone horse trough and an attendant small boy with unkempt fair hair, wearing dungarees and perched on an upturned zinc bucket. Whuppity Stoorie thought this an opportune moment to protest at the unusual length of her journey: a whoosh of steam blew from the radiator.

'Let's get out and smoke.' announced Mavor. 'This brute needs water and we can get some here. Small boy, before you ask anything irritating, could you take your bucket and fill it in that trough.'

He turned to Muir.

'And why are you going to Troon, Dr. Muir?'

'To see one of your patients, Dr. Mavor.'

'Ernest Robertson, by any chance?'

'How could you guess?' Muir continued, 'You, Dr. Mavor, gave me the idea,' Muir recollected Westermain's conversation on the Royal Scot, and later on, after the Haldane Mission, the intense young man with his engines and models, remembered from Lanark and the 1910 Air Show.

'A youth with a mission.' intoned Mavor.

But what had made them yawn in 1910 now had a certain urgency.

'The man with the seaplane obsession?'

'More intriguing than that.'

'He has got someone quite big behind him. Let me guess. Quentin Kennedy, Lord Westermain? He gets about. I think he's the only Scots politico who, apart from Haldane and now you, has flown in anything. And what he suggests is – what do you, as an engineer, or at any rate from a family of engineers, feel?'

'Possible carriers? We've only had one air war to go on. The Greek-Turk business.'

Muir elaborated on the need for protection of the convoys crossing the Atlantic from German U-Boats. Mavor said nothing but eye and mouth seemed to agree. The small boy returned with the bucket full of water, duly poured into the Argyll's radiator, which calmed it down. He was called Wullie, and was rewarded with a half-mile circuit in the dicky-seat. In another half-hour they reached Troon and a largely empty dock. Kennedy had a month's banging and clattering behind him in a corner of the place, screened by a corrugated iron shed.

'Mr Kennedy! Milord Westermain! Where aaaare yoooo!'

The equine features of the young aristo extruded themselves from the iron fencing.

'Hullo, Mavor. Pleased t'see you, Muir.'

'How's it goin?'

'Come and see.' The rusting gates folded apart to disclose further inarticulated masses of rust: parts of some Frankenstein ship banged together to do what? In the midst of it was Robertson, that white-haired boy he'd last met in Machrihanish, whose impassive near-mechanical voice rhymed out the specifications of his strange craft:

'Built Swans' Yard Sunderland 1887. North-East screw-collier

'Blackness Castle', twelve-hundred tons, two-cylinder compound engine, two hundred horsepower, steam crane. A Grierson Minto boat, bought by William Burrell, sold to us or the breakers. . . . Two thousand pounds and dear at the price.'

Westermain nodded with enthusiasm while his protégé rattled out how he had knocked the bridge flat, shifted the steering gear far aft, and put up a planked platform running the length of the vessel. 'Blackness Castle's funnel, bent and stuck on the port side with a gantry-like bridge, set up a deceptive column of smoke, coming from workers in the ship's bowels.

'Admiralty's seaplanes struggle to get their floats into the air, so no payload. Swap the floats for a normal land-plane, and gain a torpedo. Put a catapult under the decking: sort of giant crossbow. They have them on cruisers. The flight-deck's our new thing. If it works, we've clinched.'

'Mr Kelly!' commanded Westermain, and in seconds a handsome Milesian stood before them. 'This man does the spanner stuff.'

'Hath not the humblest Sanspotato the same soul as the superfinest Lord Lieutenant?'

Carlyle had asked that years ago, and Kelly – son of a Bridoonstown tenant – seemed to know the answer. Time, in its very circuitous way, had matched the estate with this hour. He briskly squired them over the 'fleet to come' before the Argyll sped them back to Glasgow.

October 1915: off Cumbrae, test flight

'Does it work?' Four months on, and Muir and Mavor were shortly to see for themselves. Lloyd George – up north – had promised his presence, then qualified 'if possible'. Not promising.

'We've waited long enough.' said Westermain. 'Blackness Castle' – prototype aircraft carrier – wheezed and clattered out of the Troon lock gates and into the fairway. An hour later she was six miles north of Ardrossan, off Cumbrae.

'We're waiting for the plane.'

'From where?' demanded Muir.

'Flying over from Renfrew. Was due to leave ten minutes ago.' Westermain flipped open the lid of his half-hunter.

Nothing happened, save the splash of the old collier rolling through the waves north towards Cumbrae. Then after ten tedious minutes the sought-after, persistent, buzzing noise.

'Here she comes.'

The sun glittered and danced on the Clyde waters. The buzz turned into a deeper, more powerful drone.

'Is this the first time?'

Westermain nodded brusquely. Then a shadow raced towards them and its noise became deafening. From their ersatz bridge just forward of the crooked funnel they saw the two-seater, its weighted wooden torpedo slung below, come in . . . slow – for they were now running with the wind – and bump down on the planked deck.

'It can't bloody stop!'

It bounced twice, rattling the planks, then the engine bellowed out again and with a dense cloud of black smoke pouring from its exhaust, it wobbled precariously into the air again.

'He's going to have another try?'

Westermain had flags and was signalling from the bridge as the plane banked low over the water and rose.

'He has to drop his speed. But without stalling. Bloody difficult. Too slow, and he stalls, too fast and he can't land.'

Again the roar of the engine and the black shadow of the plane. This time, it seemed to drop like a raptor on its prey. A kiss of smoke as it hit the planking, and – 'Mirabile dictu!' Westermain shouted – came to a stop.

'Have you met Ernest Robertson?' he inquired.

Yes.'

'And Commander Forbes Sempill?'

'*Enchante*!'

The co-pilot came towards him across the deck, hand upraised.

But a sudden gust caught the frail plane and whirled it almost across the breadth of the ship, dragging it – and the men gripping its tailplane – sideways.

Others rushed from the engine room until four were trying to restrain it. But with its engine dead the 'Zephyr' – for such was its name, in blue on its side – made crazily for the brink.

'Oh Christ, hold on! Hold on!' shouted Robertson, then 'Oh Christ! Let go for Christ's sake!' Then – 'For fuck's sake give up!'

The seamen sprang clear, rolling on the planking. The 'Zephyr's wings rose up in a semi-praying position and then the plane rolled over and fell into the sea. 'Blackness Castle' lost way and a gob of smoke from the funnel fell on the deck, obscuring everything.

'More drama than the Infirmary on a Saturday night!' said Mavor imperturbably, then desisted as he caught Westermain's distress, slumped on a Carley Float with his head in his hands. Mavor walked more meditatively to the ship's stern, eyeing the plane splayed-out on the water.

'If you had a rope that the plane could catch – pick-up – when it landed, it could come down at a higher speed and if you had weights on the ends of the rope, you could brake it.'

'We know.' said Sempill, turning to the crew.

'Can you bring a derrick to bear? See if you can fish it out? . . . Or at least attach buoys to the engine?'

Westermain flapped around distractedly, a hybrid of mad scientist and mad priest. Then looked out to the south.

'The *Metagama*. OGott! OGott!'

'Okay, what now?'

'The Yanks, Christ, I'd forgotten. They're coming over tomorrow on the *Metagama*.

Dr Mavor gestured southwards, beyond Arran, 'Or perhaps today? Might that be her?'

A column of smoke on the horizon became, in his binoculars, a biggish ship, at first hull-down, then within twenty minutes liveried in the pale grey of an Armed Merchant Cruiser, bristling with small and useless guns.

Siegfried's Journey to the Clyde

Within a further fifty minutes, the time it took for the *Metagama* to come abreast, the biplane had been hooked out of the water and tarted up. Westermain started its engine, streams of water and smoke poured out, but the propeller obligingly whirled round. The *Blackness Castle*'s hooter sounded a strangulated salute. Some figures waved from the *Metagama*'s bridge.

'Remind me. Who are these people? Do we know them?'

'They are journalists, Bismarck's *Die Reptilien*. But they're *our* creepie-crawlies; or at least our American cousins.'

When they approached the Tail 'o the Bank the journalists were decanted to the paddle-steamer, *Juno* and the smoked salmon and whisky. There were about twenty, gleaming, sharp of collar and cuff, glittering of pince-nez: and they were more reptilian than moralist.

Muir and Mavor joined them. 'They all say they know Lord Bryce of Belgium.'

'Best news we've heard so far . . . oor auld Ambassador can lecture 'em on loranorder, atrocities, the Lusitania, etcetera.'

Their cicerone was familiar. Cathy's sister Constance. Roguish cheerfulness personified as mannequin-matelot, she dashed down the companionway of the *Juno* and shepherded her charges into the saloon. The paddle-steamer *Juno*, set off full-ahead and up-river. North of Dunoon she slowed. Engineer Bob Cormack boarded from Ballantyne Muir's motor-boat.

The voyage that followed – which would have been commonplace enough to Clydesiders, particularly if hungover – seemed increasingly out of music-drama, out of *Siegfried*. Our hero's journey to the great river, with the riveters' noise rushing from the clinking rattle of their hammers: passing first Greenock and Scotts, then Port Glasgow and Lithgows –Di-din di-di-di! Di-din di-di-di! – to beat out the drums of the war effort. The *Juno*, aureate in the glow of the setting sun, pounded the evening waves. The old *Blackness Castle* limped behind, as if looking for some beach to crawl out on and die. The reporters had now been told to see her as the weapon of the future. They believed it, but Sempill didn't have to tell Muir the schedule was bust. The threat of it (he thought, consolingly) had helped force the abandonment of unrestricted U-boat warfare. A French journalist spoke: 'Lieutenant Sempill I have talked to. He has with him Baron Matsudara of the Imperial Japanese Navy, who thinks the carrier-rumour may have made Berlin cease the intensity at least of their unrestricted submarine warfare. The English admirals have now a very great deal on their plate, besides a competition for artillery from the New Army . . .'

It was back to the drawing boards for Westermain and his protege Robertson.

By Renfrew the light was hardening and slanting westwards and the eastern slopes of surrounding hills fell dark. Arc-lamps over the shipyard berths were coming on, dazzling themselves out of the river. Tugs trumpeted as they dragged a grey, government-standard 10,000-ton freighter downriver from Barclay Curle's for her trials. In the yard, fountains of orange sparks fell from rusting boxes of plates and ribs that were becoming destroyers or gunboats.

As they approached Clydebank the racket increased, and the arc-lamps stabbed at the flank of a huge ship, leaching sprays of fire: the battlecruiser *Repulse*, the world's fastest big-gun warship. For Muir it was as if Lloyd George was on the bridge with him, sibilantly hinting that he'd be wise to make terms. 'You have got so far. The dice have been thrown. Your air power miracle's run out of time, so make your deal now.' Muir thought of *Rheingold*'s Rainbow Bridge, and the Gods passing over it. And the same sort of deal being offered as enthusiastically on the Elbe or Rhine.

Ballantyne Muir's launch conveyed him to the 'Juno' to join the reporters. Muir drifted from the saloon and the journalists, walked to the prow, and poured a capful of Laphroaig, rolling it round his mouth like a wave breaking on Hebridean rock – or a woman's kiss. He lit a cigar, relished the tang as it thought its way into the slug of whisky. 'The Germans really did insult us, and they may have been right. *Das Land ohne Musik*. Not really fair, given the folk songs or the psalms.'

But here before him, in this clanging forest of steel, this vast sinister, beautiful, shaping of destruction, was something you could only think yourself into via the *Ring*. The robbery of the dwarves, the Rainbow Bridge over which . . . yes . . . his own father had crossed, from Thornfield Villa, backed up against its pit and the Monkland Canal, to Cardross with the grand Roman head office his brother had built, and Portencross, its tower, loggia and terraces stepping down to the Clyde; his lawns, trees, beloved greenhouses, their vines and tomato plants.

'Alles eitel.', Vanity, saith the preacher, all is vanity.' But that, too, was German: Brahms, in the Serious Songs: *'Und die, die Unrecht taeten, werden zum Maechtigen.'* 'And those who would do evil, become mighty.'

What mightier than to arm a nation – against this very culture. Hadn't Brahms the liberal praised Bismarck's victories? Or did it matter at all?

A young American appeared beside him, about thirty, hatless, clean-shaven, his tie hanging loose. He shook his head, and then muttered slowly, almost to himself and almost under his breath. 'Have . . . no . . . truck . . . with the senseless thing. . . .'

He looked at Muir, quietly challenging. Muir returned:

'Order the guns and kill!' then 'Your name?'

'Reede with an extra "e". Not the socialist one. *Baltimore Inquirer*. One of Kane's blatts. I'm the literary figleaf. And yours?'

'Duncan Muir. I sell the guns. We passed my yard five miles back.'

'I'm sorry, sir.'

'Why sorry? If you know your Kipling, you'll catch my feelings. And America has form in the mass-destruction business. Fifty years ago we were selling you blockade-runners. But I'm forgetting. Fancy a peg of old Islay?'

'Don't drink, I'm afraid. Mother's boy. Hannah Reede, suffragist and teetotaller? Known? Or rather, just when I was ready to throw over the traces, I ran into Jack London out of his skull . . .'

But – then – he had said 'I shan't throw away my prop just yet. What brings you here?'

'A story. Chance to travel, and so on. I missed out on Oxford, on account of Mom walking out on Pa – he was a Knight of Labor but shared Jack London's habit – and took us off to Chicago. But here I am, thanks to your swell Mr Masterman.'

Who also, Muir reflected, shared the habit of London and Reede Senior. Poor sod.

'I won't say anything. Just look. Ask the questions later. You may never see anything like this again.'

And apart from the occasional interrogative and curt reply they kept silence: 'Gunboats on your left. For Mesopotamia. Big ones are steam, named after jewels: *Scarab, Emerald, Amethyst*. Little ones are diesel and named after bugs: *Bee, Wasp* . . . By the way, should you ever rise to power in Washington, avoid Mesopotamia and never go anywhere near Afghanistan.'

'Mair Marble nor the Vatican!'

Upstream from Govan they were out of the shipyards and into the docks. Small steamers slipped west, headed downriver to the Firth and the Outer Isles and a big two-funnelled Irish turbine swept past bound for Dublin. Muir explained that the Irish seemed to be mainly onside – they had fussed enough over Belgium as Catholic martyr ran into the problem of the intense hatred of Fleming for Catholic Walloon. Holland remained neutral, as did all the Scandinavians. Reede found this odd.

'But suppose Scotland was like Norway?' Muir explained, 'would she necessarily support England? I will shortly introduce you to some people who have differing views on the matter.'

Then telegraphs clanged, the *Juno*'s paddlewheels threshed in reverse. She edged to port and the bourne of a quay, caught by old-fashioned flaring gas lanterns. 'Atlantic Quay', Muir told him. 'You can hang around here with your colleagues and wait for a cab, but they'll take your luggage to the North British anyway. We could easily beat everyone else to George Square and get some drink in to see us through the speeches.' He grinned. 'Oceans may sunder, formality doesn't change. And alcohol's the only defence against it.'

'We-ell . . .' exhaled Reede, caught both by conscience and the yellow sulphurous fog that wrapped the town centre. He saw a man waving at Muir from a shelter on the drab quay, thickset, late-middle aged, short Stonehaven pipe clamped between his teeth.

'Oh, forgive me.'

'No. I'm temperance, but not bigoted about it.'

'What you'll see may reinforce your family prejudices.'

The man said 'Duncan means a Glesca cooncillor three sheets in the wind's a gift tae the teetotal cause.'

'I didn't introduce you. Andrew Amos, my foreman.'

A rough, friendly hand grasped his. 'Thirty year here, an' it's no improved. Come oan, let's ambush the refreshment!'

They plunged into an inordinately complicated stage set, of buildings heaped on one another in a variety of architectures, whose enduring principle was intricacy; of battlements, pediments, windows arched, bow, gothic, frowning down from on high, spreading their wares, caryatid-carried balconies freighted with comely nudes shooting arches of glass at one another. Gin palaces concealing the secrecies of 'fine wines and spirits' behind frosted glass. The side-streets they traversed were cramped, cart-choked, smelt of horseshit, occasionally vomit, but of other things more exotic, roasting coffee, roasting meat, cigars, gas, occasionally the petrol of a car or the acrid cokey smell of a steam lorry. At intersecting thoroughfares huge streetcars, double-decked, whined past, and bold girls, dressed to the nines, swaggered arm-in-arm, for this was Friday. . . .

'Mind, it might no' have been you the night. Yon Hugh Stenhouse in accounts seemed awfy keen. Then he vanishes.'

'Doesn't he dae fitba practice?' Muir in the venacular.

'Somethin aboot Queens Park . . .'

'Harin' roon' it in white pants an' a semmit.'

'Men. No rational maist o' the week. Totelly gyte Setterdays.'

It was like and not like Reede's Baltimore. Buildings were smaller, apparently no dwelling-houses anywhere near this bit of downtown. And there was poverty, splayed out on the curb, whispering with a slight tone of menace, 'Ennae spare change, pal?'

Another rampart of a street had to be crossed, thronged with 'caurs' as they called them, clattering over the points, and the architectonic bravura of George Square loomed ahead. The fog had taken possession of it, and as they entered the City Chambers it surged and eddied round the huge electroliers glowing in the void above the grand staircases.

'There ye are,' said Andrew to Cathy who had materialised through the fog, impeccable in Musquash, awed despite himself, 'Mair marble nor the Vatican.'

Then round and round great whirling spirals of gleaming toffee staircase, floor after floor, finally to debouch on a landing and enter into a vast painted hall, murals featuring everything from wonder-working Celtic saints to battleships, lights glancing from even more electroliers then down and down to a black-coated throng of businessmen and councillors and a very few women.

'Ony excuse for a bevvy.' said Andrew, 'This time it's oor brithers oot west, frae John Paul Jones tae Davy Crockett.'

'Notice the near absence of the ladies.' Muir nudged, 'Though there's Kate Cranston who runs the tearooms. Bankrolls Rennie Mackintosh. Helloo!' A bright middle-aged lady in steel-rimmed specs was parlaying three bohemian-ish males, maybe artists or actors.

'Kate, here's John Reede of the *Baltimore Enquirer*, son of Hannah Reede.'

'Someone sair needed here!' She gestured at a table burdened by hundreds of measures of whisky, fast disappearing. 'If we're fighting Kaiser Wilhelm, Kaiser Franz Josef and Kaiser Strong Drink, the third's mair than got his foot in the door.'

Muir motioned Reede to an elderly man with a glare and heavy moustache and launched forth:

'May I introduce Mr Reede with an E of the *Baltimore Inquirer*. Lord Provost Sir Daniel Stevenson with a V.'

'No relation to RLS?'

'Distant if at all. Young man, you are from the USA and you work, I hear, for Charles Foster Kane. I find sensational journalism repellent, but Mr Kane at least doesn't seem to have swallowed the war frenzy. Why?'

Reede rushed in to explain about the German-Americans, the socialists, and the well-organised anti-war movement. Stevenson nodded approvingly.

'Kane seems a rough bit of work, but not as hysterical as some of ours. I hope Principal Wilson will stick to his . . . ahem . . . principles. But will you excuse me for a moment, Dr Muir? I want to see Councillor Wheatley before he goes.'

Muir shouldered Reede *sotto voce* towards a Pickwickian figure, clean-shaven, in a grey suit, looking rather distrustful of the whole *galere*.

'Get in there after him. John Wheatley's what makes things happen.'

'And Keir Hardie, where's he?'

'You didn't hear? He's ill. Dying in fact.'

Lord Provost Stevenson was arguing with a military man. Both being rather deaf, it was a loud argument.

'Stuff and nonsense! You'll take your orders from me, Sir.'

He turned to them in mock appeal.

'The Council Procession. This bandmaster wanted to play Sullivan – "Defe-er, defe-er, to the Lord High Executioner!" – from the *Mikado*. Instead of what we always have.'

'What's that?'

'Wagner, "March of the Meistersinger." '

The Provost's resolution took even Muir aback. For a pacifist, there was a bellicose glint in the old boy's eye. He hadn't endowed a Chair of International Relations for nothing.

'We are a world centre of trade and culture. We cannot indulge in music-hall posturing. My brother-in law is still Burgermeister of Hamburg. Nuremberg is a legitimate Imperial Free City. Where we might be able to get to by ploughing our own furrow.'

The band struck up, to no apparent dissent. Down the grandly-convergent staircases stepped first Lord Lyon, the Senior Scottish Herald (who actually did look as if invented by Gilbert and Sullivan in cahoots with Lewis Carroll) macebearers and beadles, then deacons and bailies, ministers and priests. Then came the military and the consular corps, the Scottish Secretary in his curious blue and gold dry-land-Admiral's rigout, the Lord Advocate, Advocates-Depute, Sheriffs, and finally the Council's best, in cocked hats, red gowns and the well-hung ermine of the Lord Provost. Surveying *Meistersinger* in the light of what he'd heard from the last, Wagner *festivus* did sound like Sullivan.

Wheatley appeared at their side.

'Ye meddle wi' Sir Daniel at yir peril. Ye're Mr Reede, Red Jim Larkin minded me o' ye, and ye'll be gettin' wise to the fact that this river's mair complex than the diplomats will tell ye or sell ye.'

'What does the Provost do?'

'For a living? He sells coal . . . but no' aff the back o' a cairt. Ye'll find Stevenson's depots in jist aboot every port o' the seven seas. Gets the stuff oot frae Ardrossan or Methil, or the Tyne or South Wales, by anything that'll float, and there ye are: moves the warld's weal on ball-bearings.'

After all this, the Minister of Munitions, Lloyd George and Colonial Secretary, Bonar Law seemed almost a plebeian intrusion. Neither was dressed appropriately, as if the circumstances of total war had accelerated official attire into a sort of civilian battledress. Lloyd George wore a short frock-coat of lovat check, with a soft collar and floppy bow tie, Bonar Law the sober business suit of a senior clerk. But while Law seemed dourly at home with the assembly, the Welshman had the air of someone released from a racetrack, alternately alert and suspicious. His eyes, Muir noted, had gone young, almost those of a schoolboy.

But it was Bonar Law who silently gestured Muir to one side.

'Adam Halley. We can get him a place in the Washington Embassy. Financial assets realisation. He has a real gift for this sort of thing. Changing his name to Andrew Henderson. I think he could be extremely useful to you industrially and to us politically.'

In the background they could hear Lloyd George getting his range. The 'little five-foot nations' bit went down well in a town which bred dwarfish boxers. Likewise the references to Harry Lauder, to Lord Bryce, to the Rangers footballer killed in last week's offensive.

'Remember that this is really new territory for Lloyd George.' Muir explained to Reede, who had joined them, 'the city may these days vote Liberal but the press was always imperialist. The socialists? That's the irony. You saw the puppet-show. Our burgh's grand conventions make the Kaiser look awfully provincial.'

Lloyd George rode this divide. Almost magically, so that he convinced supporters of both sides were left open-mouthed by his levels of persuasiveness of and engagement.

'Your boys – your tough wee boys – will be backed up by your big guns.'

He glanced at Muir and as quickly glanced away.

October 1915: A Passage to America

Half a mile away dockers had already started emptying the *Metagama*'s hold. The pulleys screeched as ropes plunged into the shadowed depths and heavy, shrouded boxes of something huge but complex were winched up into the arc-light, swung over the side, and lowered delicately on to a succession of motor-lorries.

'Turret-lathes.'

'Does Wullie Weir, Mister Munitions, ken whit you'r daen? He's no gonnae like this.' From the stevedore as Muir led his companion onto the boat.

'He's been waiting for the chance for years. Scarcely onythin' separates yon man frae the better o' his workers, 'xcept money. That's why he hates them. Y'know what the man said: "A trained gorilla could work that thing."'

As if on cue, the disembodied face of Weir, Cathcart Foundry's proprietor appeared above the hold, peering down like a small private devil.

'You'll sail in fortyeight hours, landing at Halifax.'

The grey-faced man beside Muir nodded. Adam Halley was out of prison as – indeed – Andrew Henderson. A sailor took his cabin trunk aft. Muir followed some way to his cabin, waited till he entered and when the coast was clear, quickly entered.

'Our friends may have picked you up already. Young Miss Mann was quite active. If so, they'll make contact. Move with their flow. I have men inside the US unions. They'll smooth your way.'

Henderson nodded. He had as little time as the stevedores for Weir, but thankfully Muir had got him away from this God-awful place, and poor, decent, dull Avril. The Germans now knew him as a sympathiser.

So did their Irish and socialist contacts. And in truth he was more flexible than the patriot of former days.

Henderson had dealt with cargoes all his working life, but had never been further than Tighnabruich on the boat from the Broomielaw. He knew that apparently paradisic spot, and its reality: a place replete with insect savagery: the midge capital of the West. The experience bred a suspicion of the whole notion of abroad: confirmed by a spasm of rough weather from Malin Head to mid-Atlantic that had him doubled up in the agonies of sea-sickness. His stateroom was the old *Metagama*'s best, but smaller than the cell at Duke Street. He practised his clarinet and otherwise occupied himself growing a beard. It turned out grey and rather distinguished: even though he was only in his forties: the stress of the last year had left its mark. But the result, the contrast to the uniformity of the Exchange, he found refreshing.

How to proceed? The philosophy course which then began the study of humanities at the Scottish universities proved useful in his predicament: as his nausea lessened he began to assess his position. Avril and the bairns would be taken care of: his marriage had not, on balance, been a success, but he had extorted sufficient for them. A bank account of compensation had been opened, proof enough of the guilt felt by his superiors for leaving him to take the rap.

Duncan Muir had managed to square Weir, so he must have something on him. But what did he really know of Muir? Certainly unreliable on Ireland; then there was the Bergius involvement which he had discovered from a business associate in Germany and Lord Westermain. And the women. Lady Emily had become a martyr-heroine, second only to Nurse Cavell. Muir had been reticent about this, with good reason. Cathy Aitchison he knew about. And there was Helena Mann. That peacetime evening of the Piano Quartet, she hadn't caught the tram with Bob and himself. Said she wanted to shop, though few places were open at that hour. Now she was back in Berlin, apprised of what industrial or political secrets?

Once recovered, and reassured by passing beyond U-boat range, Henderson found he could wedge himself in a corner of the promenade deck, in the lee of a companion-way, and alternating from wooden deckchair to a carley-float made up with blankets and cushions, savouring the curiously addictive smell compounded of coal-dust, steam, hot machine oil, cooking fat, wet wood drying. Beyond that the grey sea rushed past. Daily he paced three miles from forrard of the cargo-hold to the log-line at the stern, admiring the intricate massing of cabins, boats, funnel, ventilators, four-inch guns. He was given one to look after, with a couple of matelots. He served his turn on watch.

November 1915, New Brunswick: Sir William Maxwell Aitken

Halifax was congested with munitions boats, so the *Metagama* diverted to St John, New Brunswick. An awkward day pacing that low coast and coping with the forty-foot Fundy tides. While they waited for the tug the captain, with whom Henderson played chess, brought two cables. One, from the Washington Embassy announced an imminent appointment with 'William Maxwell Aitken, the press baron'. The second announced the place: the Algonquin, the big Canadian Pacific Railway hotel in St. Andrews, New Brunswick.

It took most of the day to get there by two trains, being decanted at a huge station in the middle of woods edged by lonely lakes. The Masonic token on his watch-chain, got him an unexpectedly good meal. A cab dropped him at the Algonquin in the early evening. He was expected.

'Tell you what it's about. We succeed or fail through two things: getting the USA on side, and – or – stopping supplies reaching Germany. Personally, I'm not sold on proposition one. The US and the

UK are both empires but the figures show the US overtaking us, unless we create an economic empire. I'm a Canadian. My folks didn't hang around to meet the Founding Fathers in seventy-six. They fled up here. United Empire Loyalists. Describes me to a T.'

Words sprayed out of Max Aitken's Cheshire Cat mouth like bullets. Like Bonar Law, he was out of an New Brunswick manse. Risen without trace in Canadian finance and English Tory politics. Bankrolling Bonar; probably Lloyd George as well: a noisy ideologist who made it up as he went along.

'I'll level with you, Mister Henderson. Our allies are crap. The French want a war of revenge and movement, silly buggers: running straight at enemy fire; pinned down at Verdun, a fortress they dismantled. That won't last. The Russians can't fuel let alone steer their steamroller. The Turks are causing us much more trouble than we thought; if the Russians take lessons from them, things might be truly different. Some of your Scots lefties think the next war will be the US versus the UK and they might be right.'

'So where do I fit in?'

'You have an assumed name. But the Boche knows who you are. We know that there are big US interests – not just the Irish – who want us, not necessarily defeated but weak. We want to find out who they are, how they are funded and their goals. Very few people have your view of both sides of the Atlantic. Traded with 'em. Muir vouches for you – at least while it pays him to do so. He's doing his armourers' work, but what's going on inside the helmet?

Easter 1916: Queen Anne's Gate to Ayot St Lawrence
They walked slowly along the Horse Guards colonnade while outside it the rain soaked down on the dirty-yellow gravel. The smell of Haldane's cigar seemed to Muir to recreate the political pungencies of New Year at Alderbank twenty years before: Tory Uncle Aeneas

squaring up to his Gladstonian father in the grey-and-pink parlour after coffee and whisky. Though the official Haldane was circumspect:

'How effective will conscription really be, Dr Muir?

Pfffff. A cloud of pungent Havana was there to be shared

'Are the Germans trying to probe new and possibly permeable factors? Like maybe the Irish? Will mobilising them – and women – as 'diluted' labour, work?'

The stream of blue smoke seemed to reflect the cerebration going on inside the domed head. 'Particularly after Easter in Dublin?'

'And besides this,' almost whispered Haldane, 'where do we figure now in Masterman's propaganda drive? And this war aims business the Americans seem so keen on? Enough to save us from our military?

Pfffff . . . And then with a force perhaps concentrated by suppression, Haldane hurled the cigar-butt out into the square, where it hissed and drowned in a yellow puddle, leaving a blue streamer to disperse and die.

Beaverbrook among others harried Haldane as pro-German: the other side to Lloyd George's bold capture of Munitions. He was sacked in May 1915, had his housemaid burn the *Express's* hate-mail and reached some sort of deal on background stuff with his persecutor 'in a lucid interval'. He was evaluating 'the machinery of government' so quietly a spanner's fall would have given all away.

'I don't feel mistreated yet it's "the parting of friends".'

His view of his old ally, Prime Minister Asquith, now failing and frequently drunk, was only implied, but devastating. As was his move towards Labour. Hence, Muir thought, that morning's unexpected summons to Queen Anne Gate.

'Ireland now. I'll test this on you, Muir: it's not a little provincial flare-up. I knew the place in the eighties, when we solved the university reform, the Cardinal and I, over champagne in the Palace at Armagh. Now Squiff lets that dug-out Conky Maxwell shoot a few bar-room patriots and we have the entire hierarchy *and Rome* at our throats. We expect the Irishry to troop into the trenches and – more important – the factories. Your man Westermain is of the Old Faith. Where's he in this? His carrier project's on hold: the Admiralty's quaking at a fleet action in the North Sea. Faith *might* matter more than guns.'

He produced another cigar. Muir struck a match and lit it for him.

'I can guess there are equal frustrations in Berlin. They have good people, progressive even: you can talk to General Groener. And he would be bad news for us. Knows all about logistics and is almost as big a martinet as their trade union leaders.'

They had reached the outlier of Dover House where Muir had one of his – always temporary – offices.

'Shall I have you run to King's Cross?' Haldane was en route to have lunch with Bernard Shaw near Luton.

'If you feel generous to an old man, and want for entertainment, why not have me run to Ayot – and come along? There's a bargain!'

Muir's government Wolseley coursed along the Great North Road, and the weather cleared to a metallic grey before a sharp easterly. Haldane sat silent beside him, his face under a tweed fore-and-aft hat immobile. They stopped for a level-crossing near Hatfield and a commuter train, drab black-and-brown, clanked past.

'Look, Haldane, enoughs enough. I got out of Ireland forty years ago because the place would have killed me, and since then Ive been living on my wits instead of my emotions. A great dividend to the peoples of the British Empire.

'But no more. Our little revolt provoked the British to go crazy. You can beat Germany to her knees and probably will do. You still have the factories. And then you lay yourself open to the saints and scholars, by shooting poets and socialists, teachers and bar-room mountebanks.

Martyrdom is the only way to achieve fame without talent, but some of that sixteen had talent in abundance.

'Anyway come in and have a non-cannibal lunch. You sir are Captain of Industry Duncan Muir and have at least read *Major Barbara* and are putting my speculations into action.'

Mrs Shaw presided over the sparing meal. What wasn't eaten of the nut cutlets and minced cabbage went on to the bird-table in the spring garden, amidst its cheerful drifts of daffodil and hyacinth. The grey suburban dolour of the Old Vicarage set off the umber of its proprietor's Silver Ghost, the crotal of his knickerbocker suit, hair and beard turning golden in middle-age.

'Charlie Masterman comes weekly with the massages. Will I massage the consciences of the neutrals, my American public? Bless 'em. But keep their distance from this madness. Once America gets a mission into its head, the world is in peril. Look what missionary zeal has done to the rational English.'

The bright blue eyes flickered in a troubled way. Haldane made as if to speak.

'On balance, might work. Reasons: not through politics but religion. We protestants have always underestimated the Papacy. Once spring that old man from his golden armour and make him a hero – which Carlyle was always telling us to do – he will astonish us.

'Think about this.' said Haldane. 'Suppose we get our wish and beat Germany. There are presently five great powers in Europe, not counting Turkey. Russia's all but dead – maybe in for years of civil war – and Austria will break up. Result: three great powers: Germany's objectively stronger, but we and the French will try to keep her down, so resentment all round. Small ethnic countries will be a pain, going on Italian precedents. My bet is that there won't be a single democracy among them in a decade. Worst of all is your achievement, Dr Muir. We have created the British warfare state, adept at producing – at crippling cost – every variety of industrialised destruction. Will the place ever find its way back? We have to reanimate those various national links that force people to negotiate their way, not demand it. Austria was a picturesque mess, but it held together as a democracy of sorts, with an inoffensive and quite appealing dynastic headship. We might just retrieve it by enlisting the Catholic Church and his Holiness Pope Benedict XV. *Nicht wahr?*'

At Portencross, 30 June 1916

'Are we no there yet?'

Master Colin Halley turned from the open window of the Wemyss Bay train. Trailers of smoke and steam whirled past. Below them was the lower Firth.

'Patience.' said his mother.

The two Halley girls were playing some card game, which didn't interest Avril, compared with turning over in her mind why Dr Muir might have invited them all.

'About two miles, I think. The line drops down to the sea.'

'There's anither paddler!'

They were overtaking a sleek, yellow-funneled steamer, also headed south, a white wake spilling behind her.

Avril looked into the mirror. A fleck of soot had hit her upper cheek. She banished it with a small, pink-bordered hanky. Curiosity possessed her; indeed had matured her since that morning when her husband had been dragged off by the bobbies, and then somehow disembodied and wafted across the Atlantic. She had matured, not least thanks to Cathy Aitchison, who seemed to occupy a chatelaine role at Portencross, whither they were headed.

And indeed there Cathy was, under the complexities of that wonderful

Wemyss Bay train shed, when minutes later their carriage slid into its platform.

'Hullo bairns.'

And she manoeuvred the small people through the grand concourse and out of the main doors to the Portencross car.

'Where we goin'? Is it a very big hoose?'

'Ye'll see.' Said Mr MacAulay the chauffeur, scooping them up and depositing them on the Argyll's wide red leather seat.

'I'm glad you were able to come. I hope what we've done has helped you cope.'

Cathy's efforts, she had to admit, helped a lot more than Adam had, in eight years' unspectacular marriage, largely taken up with being pregnant and nauseous. Was this life? She had tended to remark to herself, in those months when the mounting chaos of Europe coincided with an unsentimental stocktaking in the Sandhills parlour. Adam had been an escape from the Free Kirk tyranny of mother and aunt in Renfrew, but turned out to be a loner, thirled to his logarithms and his cello. Life was comfortable enough on his salary, but the third pregnancy enlisted her among the disaffected.

Then there loomed up, at the end of a wooded promontory, Portencross with its tower and loggia and terraces, and a tennis court and a path running down to a little harbour and a boathouse, and she had thank heavens brought swimming things for Colin and Maisie and wee Henrietta. Dr Muir, dapper and eloquent, greeted them at the grand door with his friend Sir Robbie Rattray, cheery moon face and an accent as broad as the Moray Firth. There was lunch on the lawn, of cold chicken with a warm spicy sauce and salmon in aspic and salad and plenty of cheesy sticks and hard-boiled eggs for the bairns, allowed, by general consent, to run wild, chase the pheasants and peacocks.

'Ye didnae build a' this?'

Sir Robbie was expansive after the picnic, rolled back in his deckchair, lit a cigar. Avril wrinkled her nose in slight disapproval, though not past having the occasional cigarette when the bairns got too much. Cathy cocked her eyes in solidarity. Duncan tholed Rattray's imperfect understanding.

'No, Robbie, the Italian style went out in the 1850s. This was Grandpa Muir's work.'

'Yon auld scoondrel? Shippit guns tae the slaveholders, shippit back contraband cotton?'

'All of us gentlemen of the West have something to hide.'

Duncan had plotted the direction of the day, and became aware that the conversation might be tending in the wrong direction. There had been a none-too-subtle purpose behind the invite. Adam Halley had gone. Spirited away from a working party out of Duke Street – that was the story Lord Clyde put about, to anyone still interested – the local plods were after him with a verve that put the Keystone Kops to shame.

Sir Robbie, now playing an elephant fairly realistically to amuse Colin and Maisie, and crashing through a bamboo grove to accompanying trumpeting and shrieking, was a national investment. Powered by tobacco and whisky, he had in weeks worked out the complicated business of ensuring milk supplies, reducing beef imports, turning pastoral land over to tillage. Lloyd George wouldn't have known what a calorie was a year ago. He did now. To Robbie calories were embodied as beeves being chugged round the country from local station to mart to slaughterhouse on goods trains, then soothed in deceptive meadows, contented and patient and calm before the brief surprise of the bolt-gun. Schedules were tweaked to aim the meat at brand-new munitions towns.

Out of the office he had become lachrymose to the point of utter gloom, comforted only by pouring 'Black and Dog' into himself after supper until he fell into bed. His Portencross stay threatened disaster, as mornings started with an unsteady pilgrimage to the cemetery to mope over 'Puir Emly' and 'Julia, ma wee lamb' (which Duncan considered a bit of a liberty, *he* was Julia's bereaved father), followed by a mid-afternoon hangover. Then Cathy, ordered down from Cathcart by cable, had come by an early train, and let Duncan 'have his wicked way' on the tower divan. Afterwards, peignoir-clad like something out of Alma-Tadema, she suggested with brisk practicality a way out.

Robbie had solved problems galore for Duncan Muir by handling Lady Emily.

'Get the hell out of here!' she had shouted from the tilting deck of the *Carnatic*.

'Look after the bairns on the lifeboats!'

That blend of fury and affection hadn't deserted Muir's mind. He had seen a quieter but no less resolute quality in Avril and it seemed that the sooner the business was concluded, the better. The longer the delay, the greater the chance of Robbie simply breaking up. So far things – animated by the three bairns – had gone well.

Duncan was in his office – phones rang every five minutes – but trod periodically across the lawn to where Robbie, Cathy and Avril were taking tea. He then retreated from the terrace through French windows to the music room, and from his grand piano came a sequence of dances out of Bach, Chopin, Grieg, etc., to which Henrietta jigged, sometimes with her grubby Animal, indeterminate of breed or gender, sometimes with her big sister, or with any adult who came to hand.

Colin interrogated Sir Robbie.

'Hoo did ye get that rich?'

'Ma faither inventit a coo.'

'Whit d'ye mean inventit?'

'Back then oor kye werna big, ye could pick them up like dugs. He bred ane that wis – ye ken an Oxo cube? – Weel, multiply yon by a million, stick a wee leg on each corner, gie it an evil temper, an ye hae Hugh Rattray's Aiberdeen Shorthorn.'

'Breed' worried Avril. Lanarkshire cousins farmed near Biggar and didn't manage to hide from her the bull doing his stuff with their cows, and Robbie so much resembled the family product. On the other hand, she had never seen him other than placid, when emotional not fierce but sad.

'Her faither was . . . ye shouldna' speak ill o the deid, but Sir Eddie hadna' a principle in his hale body. An his faither – Sir Harry, 'Hero Flashman,' they cried him – wis even worse. Ah thocht ah wis freein' Anna frae this, kind, gentle quean she was. But poor lass she'd already been condemned be yon auld brute's goings-on. First her mind, then her body. Noo she doesna even ken me. They dinnae gie her lang.'

But duties as uncle constrained mopery. He led the bairns to the quay where they boarded the dinghy for the Far Island, all of a hundred yards away, and tired out with lunch, slept in the log cabin, while Robbie guarded it from the pirates with a smokescreen from his double-barrelled pipe. Such a thing did exist.

'I'm no trying to sell you Robbie,' Cathy said as they walked down to the beach, 'but his castle, Mountbullock's the size of Balmoral and you'd like his ideas for it. It's that Robbie, for a' his coorseness – an that's pairtly defensive – is kind and actually wise. Emily and Duncan were at it like rabbits, while Robbie took care of her, as if she was some sort of marvellous gift. Which in a way she was.'

'The Baronet needs the voice of sweet reason.' And from their deck-chairs they saw how he was steadily manoeuvred through the afternoon to accept his faith and fate. Indeed the dance, if that's what it was, took place on the cropped turf of the sea-lawn, before Grandpa Aeneas' Temple to the Muse of Burns, who knew a bit about Eros and Bacchus. Against the cobalt blue of the Firth, the taurine bulk of Sir Robbie being led to the children, playing with them in some sort of martial dance, being broken to their will, seemed to conjure Avril up as some sort of female resolution, a Beltane Queen, for such was the season.

A strange, rhythmic, fervent music, sometimes lyrical as Solomon's Song, sometimes fierce as the Maori Wardance with which the New Zealand fifteen had recently scared the shit out of the Scots, thundered from the music room. Duncan had been to Les Ballets Russe and discovered Stravinsky.

So as the sun sank over the southern Firth and the whole ceremonial came to an end before them, the garlanded brown bulk part-led, part-ridden by the youngsters to the feet of the wise all-conquering Goddess of the Spring. How much was this Modern Love? How much the readjustments of the Victorian age to a world of materiality? How much a conquest by the children, with their capacity to create unity where little or none existed?

'A boy who never grew up?' Sir Robbie, collarless, wheezed before them. 'Robin Hood Rattray, Long John Rattray, any more and it'll be King Herod Rattray. Midges would be more merciful.'

Avril followed behind in secret triumph.

'You'll stay until tomorrow? There's a boat for Craigendoran at nine-thirty. Mrs MacAulay will make up cots for the children.' Who were all but asleep.

'Thanks, both o' ye.' said the Baronet to Cathy and Duncan.

The westering sun had also shone on other Scots and Ulstermen massing some six hundred miles away on the chalk downs above the Somme. Throughout the day telegrams and phone-calls about the big push had been arriving, hour after hour, in Duncan Muir's office. So far delivery was running to time; quality of product delivered was another matter. Weir wanted him in Glasgow off the first train.

In the big bedroom Maisie slept, Henrietta clasped Animal, Colin was still awake.

'Whit's Auntie Cathy mean when she ca's Uncle Duncan her fancy man?'

'Tell you tomorrow.'

July 1916: Jagdschloss Glienicke, Potsdam

Hair scraped back in a bun, dressed rather daringly in a black trouser suit, Helena Mann waited with her staff for General Groener, manager of military Germany. They had run with earlier successes and annexed a clumsy royal villa in the woods near Potsdam, a couple of cars, and a dozen or so bright sparks from the universities' geopolitics departments. The Havel stretched like a lake before them, periodically traversed by steam-tugs towing barges.

On the opposite bank reared the Gothic towers *im Englischen Stil* of Babelsberg.

'This notion ought to benefit us, Alex. After all Harcourt-Solf nearly went ahead in summer 1914: and *that* would have united our Empire with the Brits. We now know how fragile Anglo-Irish relations are, and the way these knock on in America. There is a socialist movement in the eastern cities, and much of it speaks German. Friedrichstrasse knows what it's doing when it gets a firebrand like the Dubliner Larkin over there.'

'Funny,' Helena thought, 'how daring the formerly timid on all sides become. Everyone, myself included – has nice and nasty policies. The nice ones are to do with tilting third parties this way and that, aiming at some sort of deal. The nasty ones throw more soldiers into the machinery: the war of attrition.'

They heard the sound of engines. Two big Daimler staff-cars scrunched on the gravel and a few moments later Quartermaster-General Wilhelm Groener entered, briskly and in civvies: a grey-green hunting suit, some maps or charts under his arm. Alex Birnbaum scurried up to him, cutting-out Hauptmann (as he had now become) Winfried von und zu Stumm. Helena thought Stumm's appearance bad news, though he was a guarantee that reports would go direct to his boss, Duke Rupert of Bavaria, Jacobite Pretender, Robert IV of Scotland, but she quite liked that.

The worry was that Alex as bureaucrat and Ballin as shipmaster might – as Jews who had to gain acceptance– try some demarche meant to out-trump whatever the *Generalstab* had in mind. Groener had the reputation of level-headedness, with his soft, throaty voice and sad eyes. He got on with Walter Rathenau, seconded from AEG as chief of war production, and the trade unions, like the railway manager he effectively was. But had he staying power?

'We are under what the English call Chatham House rules, so Frau Mann can I put this unsentimentally? A French officer at Sedan in June 1870 said "Nous sommes dans un pot de chamber et nous serons emmerdes." He was looking at the ring of our troops on the surrounding hills. After the Somme we are similarly placed.'

'There are two ways out, friends.' He smiled at her and she was grateful for the gesture. 'The French and ourselves hammered each other into the ground at Verdun. *They* now have only one offensive left in them. The British launched their Somme offensive to relieve them, but – and this is the difference – showed they could survive antique generalship and mediocre armament. The first may not improve; the second certainly will. Their 'tank' is capable of real development and could be deadly, within say eighteen months. As for aircraft, they can go beyond scouts. If they deployed against trains? In other words, in a totally mechanised war, can we win as a monarchy? Can we hold our allies together? If not, what other approaches are there?'

They went out of the stuffy *Konferenzzimmer* into a strange, unexpected room. It challenged the tedium of the rest of the place, as one half faced the lake, open to it with French windows, while the other mirrored it, creating if you looked to right or left infinite ranks of poplars and willows and behind them lead-grey waves.

Groener raised his eyebrows,

'We are a terribly difficult country to turn round, Miss Mann.'

Under no circumstances would you try to *dutzen* a General, but here, she thought, it might be possible. Groener's sentences weren't pronouncements, but those of an intelligent man faced with a complicated problem and eager to be guided to its centre.

'How do people speak there, on the Clyde? Are they open?'

That could be said of his own face, as opposed to the slab of meat that was his rival Ludendorff.

'Yes, but there's an intense *regionalitaet*. People "speaking broad" as they say; even middle-class folk. More difficult to follow than *Plattdeutsch* or *Schwaebisch*.'

'And they communicate across classes?'

He offered her a cigarette from a heavy brass case. She spoke more to the glimmer of the lake than to the General surveying its traffic.

'The big division is in a way between the engineers and the rest, and some of the engineers took to music, which gave me a way in. The main boss-figure I knew could switch in mid-sentence from 'received pronunciation' to broad Glasgow. The culture of the place is one of workshops, ports and making the best of strange postings, so they're adaptive. Confronting the workers didn't work, so now they co-opt; though they also slice the heads off the taller poppies. That way you don't have even to divide to rule.'

'I have read my Rudyard Kipling, Miss Mann. All about rules and how to break them . . . Think about the tank. I hear it was the idea of H G Wells, the romancer of science, then it passed to Minister Winston Churchill, whom we're quite familiar with as a military contrarian, descended from the great Malbrouck. He got the English navy to develop it when the army wouldn't. Not a chance of that here. You should see the experimental models we've tried to build. *Schrecklich*.

'As armies go, we aren't very adaptive, just as our propaganda stuff is weak. Beautifully formulated, while that of the English is maudlin. But ours goes nowhere near the heart.'

She noticed his nervousness, the fingers where he had gnawed away at the skin around the nails.

'They hold the mobilisation failure against the department. Be warned, we are smoking in the last chance saloon. Or at least I am. You are, so they tell me, doing brilliantly.'

'Hello', she thought, '*Voces intimae.*' Later and privately she thought, would such an . . .

He couldn't know – could he? – about the letters that still came from the Russian comrades via Sweden or Switzerland. Or the apartment that Karl Liebeskind borrowed, when it was safe, near the tram station, whose lights flickered through the thin curtains. Or the man, comic or satyr-like body in melancholy and arousal, the red beard brushing her belly and breasts. Or clasping her as they slept after lovemaking 'like spoons'.

Groener, eyes fixed on the barge, broke in on this: 'My worry is actually what's going to happen to our enemy in the East. Russia has broken down almost completely; our intelligence people say that there's a years' supply of English munitions at Murmansk and Archangel. Their railways couldn't move it, even if competently run. I give the Romanovs six months. If a liberal republic comes in, maybe there's the chance of negotiation, to get our boot off their throat? But even that may not be sufficient. A complete collapse, the Empire in bits, the reign of Jacobin anarchy? Some people in the *Generalstab* might want to bring that one on: I wouldn't put it past our own Napoleon, General Ludendorff to lend a hand to people he otherwise loathes.'

July 1916, Portencross

Cathy Muir woke late one August morning, having entertained rather too enthusiastically another slew of American visitors, out of boredom rather than enthusiasm. Duncan had gone straight to sleep, then crept away for a London train, without even the affectionate if perfunctory embrace she enjoyed.

She thought about men and music. The Italian operas Hugh had rather liked, honeymooning in Florence a dozen years before . . . versus the Germans that Duncan and Bob Cormack shared. That busy chorus of market-women, courtesans, etc., backing incredible heroines, balanced against introverted but believable northerners: Clara Schumann and Brahms . . . She thought about men and women, music and countries, love and loyalty. The ever-enigmatic Helena Mann and the 'child' she wrote about in her letters to Liebeskind. A desired family? A war-project like Westermain's? A socialist Utopia? These intercepted by some pliant comrade and copied – Duncan had shared with her in a brief excess of pillow-talk confidence.

'Lloyd George has a file on her which includes me. He'll use it when and if he has to.'

Around eleven he phoned.

'Look out of the window in half an hour.'

HMS *Repulse* when she came was vast and fast. Waves from her crashed on the Portencross strand like gunfire. She was already obsolete.

'Battlecruisers nearly lost us Jutland. One shot in the wrong place and their ammo goes up. They sink in seconds. But we have to commission the bugger, and the equally useless *Hood*, or else Jerry won't give up, build more U-boats. If we use the battlecrusers sensibly, we could buy enough time to get the aircraft carrier deployed.'

'Another mission?'

Duncan was thinking aloud, but it would have been nicer to have him *here*.

'Leave the shipbuilding stuff to Westermain – and Robertson, his obsessive – they can imagine progress. I can see how it might be done – but I am a mere dilettante and that's how I'll figure in the books – good on committees, trusts, etc. A sorter-outer. Trying to repair the damage, or plan for the long term. But there may be another way, at least to stop things getting worse.'

'The Americans could move our way, probably will, if Henderson can provide enough information to help us weaken any possible Irish-German fling. Dublin's Easter apart, the Irish are doing okay through munitions and food supply. Munro's wisely handing the Scots hierarchy its schools. But there's that other spectrum as Russia falls apart: from those nice ladies meeting at the Hague to Bob Cormack and his trade unionists and their links to revolutionary figures in Russia. But first things first.'

Cathy found herself striding along the beach as dawn broke. The great ship had washed it to a smoothness she had never seen. The sun caught and blushed the peak of Goatfell, almost like Hokusai's Fuji , while the *Repulse* dwindled to a smoky blur far in the south.

4

'A Poor and Sinful Creature'

'How many divisions has he?' 'Unofficial envoys,
between an elderly Pope and a young Emperor.

July 1916: Off the Fairway, Harlech

'A storm in the West, Doctor Muir. A storm in the West.'

Clouds scurried across the Atlantic and – on an otherwise clear chill Welsh day – blotched with their shadows the surface of Cardigan Bay. At Harlech, beneath Edward I's castle and a later Edwardian's big hotel, the Minister of Munitions and his entourage were playing golf. Below the battlements a special train of the Cambrian Railway hissed in the station siding, wires linking its saloon car to the telegraph lines. Its raison d'etre was the swarm of journalists, photographers and newsreel cameramen who followed – in those days respectfully – the ministerial party.

Muir was partnering Lloyd George and the press-lord Harmsworth of the *Daily Mail*, both energetic rather than elegant players, but the game was purely formal. The day's business had been fixed, and the issue to hand was making sure that the reptiles got the story they were supposed to get, the opening of a training airfield and forgot about

112

something darker, more mysterious. Only when, late in the afternoon, the last of the pressmen had retreated to train via hotel bar, did the Minister, backing to the wind, simultaneously enveloping himself in a green cloak and clapping Muir on the shoulder, call it a day.

'They go back to London in half-an-hour, thank God. Look, Duncan, look and see the storm in the West return to us. And that, my dear fellows, is why you're here.'

He gesticulated over the pebble-bank which separated dune and beach. 'We have managed, with that imperial nous for which we are famous, to wreck ourselves, well and truly.'

The Dublin business was months old. Martial law devolved power to General Sir John 'Conky' Maxwell, Commander in Chief, Ireland because reckoned too dim for the Western Front. His execution squads had done their work. Sixteen individuals earlier regarded as eccentrics were now decorating reliquaries in Dublin pubs. A mass of supposed traitors were only a few miles from Harlech, inland at Frongoch. Tim Healy MP, Irish maverick but no fool, would shortly report on how rapidly they were becoming the real thing.

'I thought for months that we managed Ireland pretty well. Peril posed by little catholic Belgium forced us to form an army of unprecedented size, and you've been arming and feeding it, but who's now bothered? Duncan my boy, this promises a labour of Sisyphus.'

Muir had never seen the boss that depressed and didn't probably help by murmuring

'And the Irish could cause infinite trouble in Glasgow if they've a mind to it.'

They made their way to the nineteenth hole and the boss continued his musings on the genius and perfidy of the Celts.

'How serious are the Irish? They're making a fuss over their martyrs now. But in a year they could settle for being on the winning side, particularly if the Americans come in. We can't coerce Ulster – we're even weaker than we were in 1914, and the Tories will get their way.

So can we do a deal? The English Tories couldn't give a damn about the place, through they'll beat the wardrums while they can. But what happens to us if we lose the Irish party? We are a moderately radical country or we ought to be after we whacked the Lords. But if we lose them, *our* Irish – and they will be a big chunk of the new voters – will sure as sure go over to Labour. The Tories will pick up the businessmen, and . . . Oh, to blazes with it. I'm tired and wandering . . .'

Healy and Harmsworth were brisk and blunt.

'Frongoch? Wales's only distillery: produced 'Jenni Jones', the only hooch that got worse as it aged. Now it's turning internees into guerillas. That young man Collins calls it a university. Knows all Shaw's plays. He can also do a standing jump over a desk.'

'Meaning?'

'If Council of Irishmen doesn't work, the Irish Republican army will.'

July 1916: Wall Street

Andrew Henderson, as we must now call him, was intrigued by the banks: initially by their sheer physical immensity, then by their detachment from any surrounding industry, their devotion to the business of Secondary Finance. Unlike the City of London which he'd visited occasionally, and its atmosphere – from the 'modern side' of minor public schools: 'Into the office at eleven, dead-drunk by four.' – the Houses in Wall Street were efficient. Thanks to the unusual female element – the secretaries and stenographers – they were *chic* as well. You entered through chambers which might have been Mycenean tombs, then elevators wheeched you up to airy floors clacketting with typewriters, patrolled by high-heeled priestesses.

One such conducted him to the seventeenth floor. Marielle: Vassar alumna, white blouse, charcoal pinstripe skirt, neat red ankle-boots. Rimless eye-glasses and just a touch of that wristy Manhattan speech. He was conscious of an appraisal that was not wholly intellectual, and didn't seem to have any European parallel – at least since the latter years of Imperial Rome.

'You imagine that because they – correction, 'we' – lend to you, we are on your side?'

In a glass-walled office-in-an-office Hector Henry Astor seemed 'off-message' as they put it. Thirty, going on seventy: as well-briefed, self-assessing, as a Rhodes scholar was supposed to be. A small, appealing figure, like a benign ancestor stolen from an oriental shrine.

'We are grateful for that.'

'Why should you be? Your people have gone altruistically into this war. My firm is loaning the wherewithal. What are my intentions? Fifty years ago they might have been bound up with religion or anti-slavery or Whitman's notion of democracy. Or the simple business of doing well by your family and seeing as many of your children survived; mourning the ones who didn't. Now they are to do with profane culture.'

'Meaning?'

'I suppose Herbert Spencer got it just about right when he argued that wealth gave us the chance to develop the senses, to revel in the whole notion of indeterminacy, and experience it on various planes at the same time. If you've enough *geld* this comedy still includes music, the arts, human relationships: whether savage or subtle.'

'I take your point.'

'But if the whole thing is simply to be regarded as entertainment, why not go back to the child? Fulfil all desires at once. Suppose you had some magic box out of which came continuous fun . . .

'The masses are satisfied enough in this way. In our specialised career, we use them as a feedstock for our own operations, but avoid rogue elements like our mutual friend Doctor Muir . . .

'A man of unease and ambition. Anxious to do good, but can't be braked, any more than he can keep himself in his trousers. In present circumstances he is more dangerous than my young traders – motivated by food and drink, girls, motor-cars. Muir has guilt. Under that dull exterior – the Germans have a word for it: *blass* – he has created a politics of challenges. These are at root meaningless but material. And because material, destructive.

'For myself I am anxious to help England because I'm not industrial. I'm a *rentier*. If I had money in Germany they'd expect me to invest in science or steelworks. But what if there's no-one around wealthy enough to buy your products? You see, we in America have been through the total war story in 1861–65. It dynamised and concentrated the economy but it didn't democratise it.'

'Couldn't you pay the workers more?'

'They'd just spend the money on more food or cheap clothes. They wouldn't either invest it or abstain from enjoyment for the longer term. That's what divides me from Jock Blenkiron – John Buchan's American buddy. His rotten digestion means he has to be a puritan.

'For me the great thing about England is that it's always been there to enable the rich to live well. Sure, it has its disadvantages. We buy French painters because nothing much has happened since the pre-Raphaelites. We invest in English heiresses and horses, rolling acres, precarious blood-lines.'

And such it was, as Henderson had found out and now recounted. The decisiveness of public opinion didn't apply. From America you woke up to the amount of actual division in Europe: the neutrals of Scandinavia and Iberia; or worse, the Balkans, a cocktail of religious and racial antagonisms that made what had happened in Belgium minor stuff. On their other hand stood the 'business of doing business': cash generated by hard-working German-Americans, instant entrepreneurs like Henry Ford, transmuted by the trading bodies and above all by these investment palaces.

There were always ways round sanctions, plans B when the UK had interdicted plan A; quiet crossings, unsupervised ports. Smuggling had marked Henderson's own family's operations off the Solway estuary, well into the nineteenth century. What had really changed?

H H Astor nodded and nodded, then interrupted this causerie by anticipating its conclusion.

'You want to ascertain if there is any truth in arms or cash leaving the US for Ireland and if so who is behind it – the Sinn Fein, Irish Americans or the Germans or a mixture of all three?'

The business of finding out would, Henderson reckoned, take him eight weeks. He looked in Astor's mirror and what he saw pleased him: 'A wee bauchle' as Seymour-Lee had once described him, 'Put him anywhere and he would just fade into the panelling.'

July 1916: the Cottage on Long Island

Ten days later a car, sent by Astor, turned up at Henderson's modest Lower East Side hotel. It deposited him at the family 'cottage' – aka 'grandiose beach house' – on Long Island for a weekend. By the Saturday evening (surveying matters from one practical direction) he felt himself ripe for a nervous breakdown. The place in its well-tended woodland looked antique and he realised *was* antique, having come across in crates from the old world – bits of Sussex farmhouses, Wiltshire rectories, aristo *Hotels* from the Paris Marais, carefully restored until it was in some way more authentic than its European prototype: partly by replicating the sheer mindless affluence of its *ci-devant* possessors. Through it drifted an affable crowd from Wall Street and its ganglions: money made material as luxury and pleasure, eager to please, cultivated within limits, deeply ignorant of the material lives it had acquired, whether in European trench or factory, on a long-term or short-term basis.

From the edge of this, in his black dinner suit, a glass of chilled white wine in hand, Henderson parlayed his endlessly supplicant hosts as if in some persistent dream, evolving on the *qui vive* a succession of social skills that removed any literal, identifying content from his discourse.

Blenkiron – Astor's right hand man – materialised beside him.

'You are bored, my good fellow. So am I.'

Yet he agreed with the shambling old man that all the time he did find himself mysteriously alert; both men having become 'wired up to' the ambient tones, off-cuff remarks and opinions; waiting for a hint of the possible future direction of this great amalgamation of peoples. Here on the surface was society: destinies which drew the ambitious along a realistic path to status and security was worth tapping in to. Everywhere agreeable contacts, the management of new careers – while the cumulative experience of the upper world was like being rushed headlong into the unknown by some creative genius. Blenkiron was off the next day to Europe. Henderson wanted out but not quite yet.

Charles Foster Kane presented himself.

'Do I know you?' he said.

Young, dinner-jacketed and balding, face in the fixed rictus of a carnivore grin, Kane moved through this fluid world like a shark. Henderson had encountered his newspapers while at work in Glasgow. The name was Protestant Irish a long way back, the man about thirty-five, his wealth suddenly inherited; his understanding of the new journalism self-generated, comprehensive,

'Not just these football teams, bankruptcies, divorces, patriotism, etcetera but getting the stuff by pictorial telegraphs, over ticker-tape. Knowing stock-prices, club-cars, ocean liners. Growing our brains, till we become like H G Wells's Martians?'

The big liquid eyes regarded him: supplicating? calculating? Henderson didn't know.

'Each not only with their own timetables but with their own society, defined by new laws of caste and frontier.'

All this came through ten minutes of breathless exposition – a vast panoramic paragraph of subordinate and qualifying clauses, saved from incoherence by Kane's puppy-like winsomeness. Henderson inter-jected occasional guidance-phrases, had them welcomed. The Kane train-of-thought rattled along a different line, working matters out for itself. His slant on the German, Irish, American nexus – that it would disintegrate apart from a handful of zealots making noises off. Henderson: because Britain has an empire and the Germans didn't?

'While Imperial Britain is vocal in Fleet Street, but not necessarily patriotic?'

'Interesting. Interesting. Give my regards to Messrs. Hamsworth and Keith Murdoch, when you see them. I see Aitken this side frequently, and he's promised me more than a word with Haldane.'

The smile flashed on like a lighthouse.

'We must in due course meet. My card . . . Ah Barone, Principessa . . . Mr Andrew Henderson, of Glasgow, Scotland. Tancredi, Barone di Falconara, Italian Minister, the Princess Casamassima, of Florence . . .'

September 1916: Baie de la Somme

The creature slowly lurched up and down over great waves of fern and heather, leaving in its wake a slick of glutinous brown mud alternately churned-up and smooth. Occasionally the left track would stop and the right continue and it would veer leftward; or vice-versa. Inside it was stifling, cream-painted, and reeked of diesel.

'This one's father.' Evidenced by the erect three-inch gun protruding from its barbette.

'The other's mother, which has only a hole for her Maxim-guns.'

'They're called machine-gun destroyers. We call them tanks.'

When Kitchener drowned on 5 June, Lloyd George became War Minister. He resented that, though he reckoned he'd ridden out that awful mid-year of Jutland and Somme Day One. The tank reminded him of a saying – drifting in from pre-war reading on Germany – '*Es lauft*' – 'It's going our way.' And he had also acquired the vivacious girl in the tweed skirt, Aran jumper and white tammy as chauffeuse, etc.

'That Tietjens business? Yes, he's out to get me, on those army calculations. An old-fashioned Tory, but German blood in him. Sylvia Tietjens – they may or may not still be married . . . a *Shinner* bound up in the Dublin Rising . . . mad as a bat, and vicious!'

The minister lay extended, and after hectic battlefield touring and his new girlfriend's energetic efforts, fairly exhausted on the bed in the Hotel des Amis, Abbeville.

'Mustn't make a habit of this. Have to be on guard all of tomorrow, young Geddes takes me round more trains.'

For much of the previous day Constance had been his driver in and out of the northern Somme front. As if decanted from a Christmas box, new clipped-together rails had been pressed on to brushwood mattresses and along them diesel shunters propelled high-explosive shells and cases of small arms ammunition, sandbags, barbed wire. General Geddes came part of the way. A small bland man who seemed like the manager of a London department store and, when he took off his greatcoat, was dressed in civvies, his business pinstripes jammed awkwardly but functionally into airman's boots.

Then they parked the saloon car on a limestone bluff that looked out towards the Baie de la Somme and Le Touquet and discussed. After Clifford's wounding at Loos, Lloyd George had consoled her. The news from Nottinghamshire was not promising. Clifford was losing himself on the Coal Commission, and she realised that much of what was said of Dai was true. The previous night he had been virile, expert, and affectionate. In the midst of this frightful war they were like a conspiracy of two against the world.

'Back in May Charlie Masterman drove me from Oxford to the Wharf, near Abingdon. We went to see Squiff, discuss some sort of deal that would leave him in charge of the home front while I took on got the war and the military.'

'Squiff argues – shilly-shallies more like – about conventions, *amour proper* and so on. Easy to see he doesn't want to bloody budge.

Scared to take the initiative cos he'll get blamed, quite content to leave the show in their hands.'

She remembered days of exhausting technicalities exchanged between the old brigade and licketty-spit staff officers who ignored her so totally it was comforting. He did not.

'Lie on your tummy.' He said.

He slipped his hand down her bare back and kissed her between the shoulder-blades. 'Bum, buns, po, *derriere*. We are unromantic about it, the French are not.'

'Where do you get such information?'

'State secrets. No. My friend Monsieur Albert Thomas, the French munitions-minister, a romantic Socialist, has a very attractive *petite amie* . . .

'Poor old Squiff, married to Margot. Delightful in her way, and another Glasgow lass, like you. But a little of her goes a long way. Squiff evidently thinks thus. Scares us all by writing reams to that Stanley girl.'

'Oh yes. And a present from Albert's girl . . .'

He rummaged around in a despatch case and produced a frivolous cardboard envelope tied up with pink ribbon.

'A new French invention, perhaps as deadly as the tank. Just out of the fashion labs of Paree.'

It was also pink, tiny and lacy, but she saw immediately what it was for.

'What's it called?'

'The French call it a *soutien-gorge* – supports the throat. Meaning it does the pull-em-up, push-em-out business of the corset, without the whalebone torture. I think it might catch on. Milner, who has unexpected expertise here, says the *Vie de Paris* bunch at the front call it a *brassiere*, after the lifejacket. Will that do the trick?'

'My God, you are what my lefty friends call the great commodifier.'

'Eh?'

'Meaning, you Welsh weevil, you have everything calculated to the last cent, including things that can't and shouldn't be calculated. Me, I assume, included.'

He creased into a huge, Cheshire cat-like grin. So she went on,

'Realise this, *mouche*. Your war has truncated my sex-life. My virile Clifford is now a neutered but energetic tomcat chasing rats (mostly freens o' mine) out of the coalfields. But as that French actress said in 1870 . . .

Said what?

They accused her of sleeping with the Germans, "Ma coeur est pour la France, mais ma con est pour le monde."'

'I think I get it. There's an awful pun there.'

Later and clothed, she reflected on this *braverie*. He could have her arrested on some letter de cachet, tried by *francs-juges*, shot or strangled in an *oubliette*. But the fact that all these fates were in French, and not in healthy, open-faced English, reassured her.

November 1916: Whitehall

'Rationing? . . . coupons . . . ? Sir Robbie – *pronto*! He's settled down well. Deputy Food Controller under Rhondda. When my Emily died – they were close, y'know – he needed something that kept him working 26 hours a day. The boss found it for him.'

Muir was telephoning, smoking his fourth cigarette of the morning and drinking a paper cup of foul coffee extract in a corridor at the Commons. Lloyd George had taken over the title of War Minister on 9 July, after Kitchener drowned. His late wife's companion was still given to fairly extravagant displays of grief, though at strict intervals and after good dinners in Soho. After a quarter-hour of sobs and hankies Muir brought him some logistical problem. Sir Robbie's aptitude in solving these he recognised as a bequest from Emily.

As he dwelled on that thought a cable printed out, about anti-submarine experiments in Fife, signed E. Rutherford, which jogged another memory-stream. Back in the nineties Emily's tutor had gone to St John's Cambridge, and became at twenty-five a College Principal in New Zealand. He was rarely mentioned – for those years her voluble diaries were absent. Had something happened? Nun-like she was not, nor equable, but she had helped reconstruct Ballantyne Muir, and she valued the young physicist, predicted by H G Wells. 'To split the atom of certain elements, releases energy of *unbelievable destructive force.*'

He had found himself alternating between being Emily's keeper and interpreter, distracted by her devotion to womens franchise and a host of other causes, but also empowered. What had come together in that ornate Dumbarton boardroom of Ballantyne Muir Ltd., or around the dining-table at Portencross, was humanist and modern.

Could it sustain itself, or would it grind itself – as much as Germany – to bits? In that alien London corridor he started to reorganize the questions raised in high summer days when he steered *Dalriada* from Portencross to the works. The boat wasn't white-winged escapism, but was like an office entailed on him by his father. Guard-dog and way in and out of a natural world, a priest-hole from the terrifying calculations of the Munitions District – but with access to Lloyd George, Watson Wilson's transcripts from the arsenals, Con's sporadic phone calls giving some notion of Lloyd George's strategic ploys. These days his own efforts now seemed to counterbalance the increasing mechanisation of the world he was forced to live in. MacTaggart's painting 'The Coming of Columba' captured white boat and sails, strenuous gospels: in the midst of this, with the frantic convolutions of the Books of Kells and Durrow in mind, not just the impressionist joy of sunlight on water: but a kingdom, foolishly lost, to be retaken.

November 1916: Troon to Westermain: the Kennedy Cause

The *Blackness Castle* business was months back. Impressions had been made, wheels set in motion. The conceptual gap left by the collapse of the Dardanelles business had been filled by the 'plowtering aroon' of

Muir and his confederates on the Clyde (all right, in most of the industrial areas, but somehow radiating from the Clyde). New organisms – seaplanes, minesweepers, these monstrous tanks, but also small, deadly things, like the Stokes mortar – were growing, but in the mountainous shadow of high-explosive shell.

Not least in a sort of 'privy council' way: with women like Frances Stevenson, Lloyd George's 'London wife', becoming a power in the land. It was, Lloyd George found himself telling Muir and Herbert Fisher – University Principal and historian, and a coming man – like 'Shakespeare's England running in reverse.' He was Queen Elizabeth – also pretty much Welsh – and these busy and confident women were the new Cecils (Welsh, too) and Walsinghams: first thrown around him, now beginning energetically to grow on their own. Frances was almost 'Old Guard'. Muir's Cathy had effortlessly passed him (starting at that big Glasgow bash) on to sister Constance – she emphatically didn't use her title – who joined his entourage as 'someone else for fun'.

The pioneer aircraft carrier didn't survive its luckless debut, and had by the years' end been melted into so many howitzers and shell-casings. Robertson was sidelined into one of Christopher Addison's research outfits: Rutherford's at Aberdour. Lord Westermain rejoined his Territorial battalion. A bloody, wasteful and doubtfully conclusive minor offensive had been arranged to divert attention from the internment of the 'Southern' Front in Salonika and increasing problems in Russia. A bullet-smashed shoulder took Westermain back to Scotland and the stasis of a mobilised but directionless Clyde. He cabled Muir, dumped momentarily at Portencross: 'Come down to lunch please at Westermain. 12.50 at Girvan will be met.'

And there he was, the man himself on the platform. Alternative notions fulminating away.

'Altogether elsewhere, ideas about carriers *are* getting somewhere, not under the old team but young Sempill and his Jap friend are hovering around and have their beady eyes on the *Furious* y'know – the daftest of old Fisher's light battlecruisers. I'm on a quite new dodge. Might just get us off the Irish hook.'

The estate cabriolet, a big black Arroll-Johnston, butted through a south-westerly which was was whipping the Clyde on to the Ayrshire coast, booming in the already wind-bent plantations, splaying the sheep-cropped grass on the hills, rollocking the dark, heavy-leaved rhododendrons, even agitating the mown lawns of Westermain. The car stopped a hundred yards short of the East Front, and they descended.

'Does yir heid in, but?' Quentin Westermain's vernacular, even modulated by Ampleforth, was odd but accurate. The vast building that confronted them seemed, caught by the gale, to summon and emit music. As they paced towards it, something out of a Bruckner adagio welled from that repetition of window and chimneys, tower and spire.

Music alone could not capture colonnade after colonnade, loggia and battlement rising on battlement, roofs and towers in pink sandstone caught in the forenoon light where the enchanted woods met the Firth. This was reverential, a palace for a scholar: the withdrawn saturnine figure who stared from the Watts portrait, who had figured in a Disraeli novel, spent as much as Ludwig of Bavaria on palaces and music: not in credulous *Mitteleuropa* but in douce Scotland.

'Overwhelming it is', offered Westermain, walking haltingly and carefully up the balustrades which gave on to the bay. 'I only remember him as a dark shape – though not frightening – who would give me pocket money. But one afternoon, perhaps he had nothing better to do, he took me through what he called the children's castle: a sort of parallel place that only little ones could understand, where there was Joan of Arc hearing her voices and the Blessed Bernardette seeing the Virgin, and Hansel and Gretel and the wee boy meeting the *fause knicht* upon the road.'

'Where were these?'

'In stained glass, in paintings, in little sculptures. Most of them I've lost track of, because it was all magic and he died not long after. I didn't want to break the spell. He did all the voices.'

It had always taken Muir some time to follow the tortuous nature of Quentin's belief. The social element seemed the same as that of his Independent Labour friends. Rather like Keir Hardie's mysticism, except that there was at its core an idiosyncratic, very catholic God whose providence expressed itself through eccentric miracles: effect wasn't necessarily preceded by cause. At one level he shared the credulity of Irish or Italian peasant women and their hunger for numinous places. Commonplace stuff. On another he now seemed a servant in this place, wore the clothes of a workman, had gone to the war as a private.

'I took a commission out of sheer fury. I could pull some rank on behalf of my men when the Staff really lost it. I think they liked me for it. I never had greater kindness than from these men, though only a few could even read. I wasn't prepared and they knew it. One of them saved me. He said "Throw away yon fuckin' pistol. The snipers'll spot ye by it and blaw yir heid aff. Carry a rifle an' they'll think ye're wan o' us."

Westermain looked from the loggia out to the firth and the service steamer that came over it. It came much closer to the shore than usual, and without stopping, prepared to lower a motor-boat. Off Kerrycroy it slowed, and the motor-boat sped towards the shore. Ten minutes later Muir heard a car deposit someone in the porte-cochere. 'That's our man. Change of plan. No more machines: Remember Dublin, and make up a list of remarkable men.'

By this time Muir had lost his concentration – as he used to do quite frequently with Keir Hardie in spiritual mood, Swinburne's paganism coming to mind:

God, whom we see not, is: and God, who is not, we see:
Fiddle, we know, is diddle: and diddle, we take it, is dee.

The voice of Viscount Haldane restored him to full consciousness.

'I may have found us an approach to the Irish problem – for a start. Mobilise the Holy Mother Church.' he said.

'Snap!' answered Muir and Westermain in unison.

December 1916: Morningside, Edinburgh, Father Gray

But first it involved Muir in the Purgatory of Catholic diplomacy, and an appointment with the Nuncio in Glasgow. The heavy furnishings of the Central Station Hotel – by the architect of Westermain but in *spiritus mundi* – coexisted uneasily with the purple and black of the middle-aged, blue-jawed, brisk Monsignor Carracci. It was all but impossible to empathise with the abstracted professionalism his caste exuded. The chosen children of quiet provincial Duomos in the old Papal States, with their baroque palaces, containers for the careers of sons of great landowners or their *avocati* settled around colonnaded squares in the grey-green shadow of the Apennines. The Vatican differed only in being even more withdrawn: warding secular Italy off for over forty years, since Napoleon III's French guards cleared off to be shot to bits by the Prussians at Metz or Sedan.

Who among his eminence's acquaintance might know a way in?

Caracci's comments were at first mere *blague*.

'I am sure that if His Majesty's Foreign Secretary Lord Balfour might manage to talk to Count Czernin . . .

'If the Holy Father were allowed to mediate an agreed settlement in Ireland . . .

'If France and England could agree on the guardianship of the Holy Places . . .

'If the French President could countenance the confederal reconstruction of Austria . . .'

'As if, friend, as if. But there is someone. A long shot.'

'Father Gray.'

'Who is he?'

'Priest of St Peter's, Morningside.'

'That Gray? I had quite forgotten . . . The portrait in the attic?'

'I don't think he would like to be reminded of that. He has a European mind, travels extensively. His friend Monsieur Raffalovich is brother-in-law of William O'Brien, deputy-leader of the Irish Party. Speculates much about the evolution of Vatican external affairs.'

So Muir travelled to Edinburgh Waverley by train, convoying well-set lawyers back from increasing and lucrative Glasgow assignments, making fun of their clients' vulgar new wealth but pocketing it nonetheless. He scrambled up the Waverley Steps on to a sleety Princes Street and waited by the kerb until a subterranean rumble announced that a cable car was coming. Twenty minutes later the same antique set him down on douce Church Hill, each corner it seemed guarded by a different denomination of church.

Many years had passed since Gray and his companion Andre Raffalovich had deserted from the Decadence and been converted to the Faith. Willie Yeats spread the story that they were on a black yacht, with black sails, called *Iniquity* when they had heard a priest gabbling mass to crones on a semi-deserted Mediterranean islet, and 'went over' there and then, renouncing the Yellow Book and the lilies and languours of vice for social service in cold and windy Edinburgh, albeit in a charming Italianate church and presbytery by young Robert Lorimer.

'I see what you're driving at, but you've left it pretty late.'

The beauty that had entranced Oscar Wilde was now a businesslike senatorial middle age: thinning white hair, pince-nez.

'You've read that book of Corvo's Hadrian IV, sensation of 1904?' Muir nodded.

'Man was mad, of course, but some bits would work. In peacetime, but we're not there.'

'I was afraid you would say that.'

'What is happening is bloody. Andre and I have that young man

Sassoon here quite regularly from Craiglockhart Hospital, so I know at first hand. The problem is that bad though the situation is, the alternative is often much worse.

'The Habsburgs look, comparatively speaking, good, but they privileged the Magyars and fiddled around pitting one group against another in the Balkans. Lloyd George is encouraging the Greeks to imperialise in Asia Minor, and both the Arabs and Jews to run Palestine . . .'

A heavy, studded-leather, door swung open and two young men came in, one in uniform, the other in a black tunic.

'Dr. Muir, do you know Captain Scott-Moncrieff? Translating Marcel Proust, so is apprised of what happens in Paris. And I think you already know Lucas Kelly, of Bridoonstown, Donegal?'

So this was where he'd got to after Glasgow? He had heard of him in Jacobs' Biscuit Factory at Easter, along with Eamon de Valera. Where were the wife and weans? But here he was, looking almost a priest, and in some sort of diplomatic intrigue.

'I have a telegram from your man.'

Gray took it, clipped his glasses on his nose, raised his eyebows, nodded. Muir noted that his cheeks now had a patina of little pink veins – lightened by powder? The toll the Edinburgh weather took. Raffalovich's Swinburnian curls were streaked with grey. He took the cable from his friend, then passed it to their guest.

'There from the Apostolic Nuncio at the Vatican: we have our *congé*.'

Spring 1917: Henderson in the Maritimes

It took only one more social weekend on Long Island to make Henderson conclude that alcohol and uninformed goodwill was the order of the day and that Astor's conclusion carried even if the route to it was less than profound. Making it a choice of either the Astor Cottage or him. He ducked out of what festivities he could and managed to walk across the Island, trying not very successfully to gauge a place transformed by the international style of affluent tourism. Then he spotted masts and funnels to the north and at Sag Harbor found a small cargo steamer and learned in a bar it was bound for St. John and took a few passengers. A bit of haggling would see him (as sole passenger) landed at St. Andrew. He cabled the Algonquin Hotel to keep his luggage, lied blind about family illness to Astor, and reached the little port ahead of sunset.

The SS *Richibuctonia* took two days to make the trip, enough time to formulate in a rough way the sort of issues that his evidence had disposed his mind to assess. He made out a series of cards and assembled them in patterns on the unused dining table. He messed with the three officers. Their opinions didn't inspire complacency. Europe was far off. But Wall Street, almost visible, and Organised Labor, encountered daily, inspired even less trust. If he had expected that the nearness of Whitman's Pawtucket or Thoreau's Walden would inspire high-principled discussion, nothing was doing. Off St. Andrews the *Richibuctonia* signalled for a tender and a perilously small dinghy took him and a large trunk to the pier.

He stayed a night at the Algonquin and asked about furnished properties on short lets in the little town, which had literally 'swum over' the Sainte Croix River from Maine in 1783, the Loyalists rafting their houses across. The old schoolhouse turned up, whose Bostonian owner was with a Friends' Ambulance Unit in Italy. He laid out the main room to take all the documents and press cuttings, which arrived by rail in his cabin trunks. Blenkiron had given him a calculator powered up by accumulators which he swore by, and a dinky typewriter. Astor had given a watch-fob token (in gold) for first-class railroad berths, to wherever. Aitken had promised him help from his finance people, if he needed it. The big hotel would provide cables and rooms for anyone who wanted to visit.

He intended to ask some general questions: from the point of view of an American *homme moyen sensuel*, seeking to turn the situation to personal advantage. Blenkiron, visiting in September, found him pacing along his table, with envelopes containing data which he had worked on, adding to an agreeably complex 'patience-like' pattern. Initially, these were to be 'propositions' in white with positive responses in blue, negative in red.

They sounded like Anglican antiphons:

Could European motivations work to get the US into the war?

But would business pressures balance them?

Were the Irish Americans running guns to Ireland to destabilise the British war effort and were they being helped by the Germans?

The shipping lanes not only needed protecting for grain supplies but to prevent the enemy getting in the backdoor.

US Steel, Standard Oil and Ford were bigger than anything British.

Where did their authority end? How were they being affected by the war?

By profiteers in Britain – making them cheaper? By profiteers in the US – retarding them?

How was political pressure being brought to bear?

Directly through commercial institutions, particularly arms firms? Or through markets/communities?

How did migrant groups from Europe react?

French? French-Canadians? Slav? Would they be positive?

Scandinavians, Blacks, Jews: socialist-pacifist?

German, Austrian, Swiss: hostile?

And to what effect, compared with capital?

Further hypotheses: a rhetoric of patriotism, but for how long?

After profiteering and overcharging? After reasons of state had been used to coerce Labor, not Capital?

Could such arrangements survive hostilities?

The Chemical Bank linking Brunner Mond and I G Farben, the

Cantinieri-Coats Cotton cartel?

Finally, and autobiographically, how much was this deflecting his own career? Keep on adding the material. Log and synchronise the cases, the comings and goings, activities in the City and Westminster, Wall Street and Washington.

The process of filing and calculating was supposed to last about two months. The Algonquin helped. A cable had arrived from Helena Mann: involved through Groener with the Soviets, but perhaps eager to run her own show?

'You know Miss Mann is involved with Kuno Liebeskind? She is extremely discreet, covers all her tracks, he even so.'

Blenkiron was surprised, he had always regarded Helena as devoted to the German cause. But Henderson, alert to the communities of neutral capitals, could always distinguish between 'nationalists' and 'welfarists'; thought of her as what chemists called a 'free radical'.

Who in Europe could sound her out? They thought of Muir, but by then he and Buchan had other ploys.

And there the record ended. Henderson typed up the heads of information and despatched them in a short report to Lord Haldane via the diplomatic bag. The full version and the archive were supposed to go to Spring-Rice at Washington. But the Admiralty had already got hold of the cables which would bring the USA into the war on April 6th. Earlier communications were quickly swamped by the business of kitting out the alliance. By the end of the year Henderson and his material had, as Buchan wrote, 'leaked out of the landscape'. Deliberately? Had he 'dived under' as the Germans put it? Or been killed by enemy intelligence? Or was he in Halifax in December 1917, when the place was blown apart?

Anyone's guess.

May 1917: the Villa Aschenheim, Zurich

'. . . As for Vienna, it will survive, however incredible that may seem. An engaging, enterprising brain attached to . . . nothing.'

Despite being of the party, Mr Somerset Maugham was sceptical. He was sceptical about most things, but about the preservation of the Danubian monarchy most of all. He held court for respectable Zurich in the rusticated arbour which terminated the garden of a small, delicate white villa, a hundred feet above the lake and a hundred yards from the tram stop. Westermain and Muir fell in step with a young Swiss officer, both unsure of exactly where or what the Villa Aschenheim was. Matti Bauer we have met. An energetic Frauenheld whose pretty companions (including Connie) the former British attaché had patronised to disguise tastes which were not exactly *comme il faut*.

Little London newsprint had been expended on Switzerland, but more than in Glasgow, which seemed on a separate planet. Absence of a Swiss merchant marine accounted for that. Quite what Maugham did was mysterious; he was supposed to be 'keeping an eye on' sundry foreign malcontents domiciled in the place, particularly Russian social democrats; but it was unclear whether this was merely a front to disguise his main concern – the noted attachment of the Swiss military establishment to its German instructors. Muir found himself under a quiet but less than discreet observation, from which it proved relatively easy to escape.

Matti Bauer's dalliance with Constance Reid was far in the past

'Where did she go?'

'Back to bloody old England. Where her father – in his heart of hearts – wanted her. Married one of his sitters, Clifford Chatterley, coalowner baronet from the Midlands. Not an oaf. Collected Whistler and Sickert. Now Con queens it over his rolling acres and buried black gold. She could exercise *Droit de Madame* over all these brawny miners, and it wouldn't surprise me if she did. She was an eye-opener, that girl.'

On the edge of some boxwood-hedged rosebeds, an old man in a pale frock coat was regarding them with some alertness. Grey hair cut *en brosse*, a trim black beard, high-buttoned waistcoat, white stock.

'Connected with my old opponent and later fast friend, Otto von der Gruenewald, were you not?'

'You must be . . .' Westermain replied but was cut off.

'Friedrich Count Gondremark.'

Muir found this baffling. Westermain did not. In his pious circles the Gruenewald crisis of the mid-1880s was still aktuell, even if their interlocutor was probably its last survivor: the pocket Bismarck of the southern States who had evicted his apostolic master in favour of . . . well . . . a Prussian Staatsstreich. Prince Otto corresponded with the Marquess of Kintyre, one mad castle-builder to another, and had died in his Fiesole villa a decade earlier; he remembered his slender, distracted widow murmuring friendly nonsense, floating around a crush at Kintyre House during the present King's Coronation. Gondremark's mistress, people had said. She would be how old, now? Pushing sixty?

Time establishes our distances, Muir thought. Zurich was scarcely eighty miles south of Gruenewald.

'Why are you here, Quentin Kennedy?'

Gondremark was not a man you lied to. Still, wait . . .

'My guess would be that, in some way, you represent the ingenuities of Milords Lansdowne and Haldane, though you are well and truly inoffiziell and you have not the slightest idea of the mind of your British government and the strange peasant genius who has come to lead it. I went to that Exhibition in Glasgow in 1888 when I was "on my travels". It was as if from another planet, but it was the world of Mr Lloyd George and his friend Mr H G Wells, something run up by an uncle from the little farm, who had seen New York and set his foundry or shipyard to work on a model of his future. It was fascinating but dangerous and you had no idea of how, if anything went wrong, you could stop it. That is where you are, and you have come to us, the functionaries of an ancient empire, to see if we know where the brakes are. But we've forgotten.

And he smiled his Mephistophelian smile.

'Possibilities and personalities in Germany?'

'You never can tell.' Gondremark produced an ambitious leather cigar-case, took out a seven-inch Havana, and lit it from a matchbox labelled 'Scottish Bluebell'.

Where, thought Muir, had he got that?

'In my time, there was some independence in the Bundesrat. There are people in Bavaria and Wuerttemberg who see the war concentration as increasing the power of Berlin and destabilising their Biedermeier princelings. Can we regenerate that old order, Mr Muir?'

Gondremark gazed out across the lake. A small white steamer had set out from the Hoergen shore. A plume of steam was followed by the low tone of its whistle. Before it skittered small yachts, sailing dinghies.

'Let me put it this way. The bloodbath that ended last November on the Somme was distressing to you in England, partly because your strategy was incompetent, and your artillery faulty. But your forces kept on coming, which our high command had not, I think, expected, least of all those 'tanks'. My young friends in the Wirtschaftsministerium had not picked up the remarkable switch of investment in your industrial economy. We had not expected it. Berlin is already pressing on its sources of supply. Incoming cargoes are being impounded in Holland and in Denmark. We have suspended unrestricted U-Boat warfare, but the vice has been tightened. You have drawn on your international contacts in insurance, forwarding, oil supply.

'There is a party in the Reichstag which might favour negotiation. But there is a larger one, connected to Colonel-General Ludendorff, which seeks to intensify a harsh militarisation. Ludendorff has, in alliance with Grand Admiral Tirpitz (and that's new) augmented the country's U-Boat fleet. I would expect that they will shortly take the risk of commencing unrestricted warfare against all vessels heading for, or from, British ports. They have even managed to persuade Albert Ballin to including this démarche in the Kriegsmarinestrategie, poor man.'

'So?'

'We approach a point of balance, my friend. Your great weakness is Russia. Ours is your unexpected war industrialisation. Your intention is, I fancy, to detach Vienna, my Emperor, from the Central Powers, but is it the intention of your government? And have other governments not got other ideas?'

Gondremark peered over the white stucco balustrade.

'You see that little boat down there. A month ago I was on it, and a party of Russian social democrats – names 'Lenin', 'Trotsky', for what that's worth – were at the next table, with friends and others. They were quite noisy, and one said, "If this little tub were to sink, the Russian revolution would sink with it." Their dream was to travel via Berlin with safe passage to Russia. You see, my friends, while you were indulging in Western fantasies of US led conspiracies, the Germans have seen to it that your ally in the East is destabilised. A Monday later they had gone. No-one knows where.'

'And that conversation had been in German?' concluded Muir.

'You may have got my point.'

June 1917: Rome, the Pope of Peace

Young Westermain's sincerity and old Gondremark's plausibility were such that Muir was within hours enduring a day and a night on a Wagon-Lit. Then he was in Rome, morning-coated, driving to an appointment with Monsignor Pallanzi. The slightest suggestion that some diplomatic demarche – even an accommodation – might be possible, once in Westermain's hands, opened doors, booked tickets, deposited him in a bedroom in an otherwise chilly family villa among the cypresses of the Parco Apostolico.

Pallanzi, Federigo. The record was impressive and so was the Vatican diplomat. 'Someone said that Federigo was Machiavellian; but at least you knew where you were with Machiavelli. He is the absolute diplomat. If anyone can restore the Old Europe, it's him.'

A car came for Muir early, and drove him westward to a small monastery, in a grove of parasol pines, high on the slopes above Trastevere.

The Monsignor was in clerical mufti, a high-buttoned black suit and white tie, like a Victorian clergyman of Trollope's day: clean-shaven, balding, as austere as a Free Kirk minister, though his manners wore the silk of the Venostas. He piled a log on the fire which enlivened a room seemingly unvisited for centuries, sixteenth-century murals fading on ochreous walls. An old woman served crisp rolls and more than drinkable coffee. Pallanzi offered a cigarette.

'You were in need of a holiday, Dottore, and where else to come but Rome? I have observed your city's genius for invention and in producing weapons of destruction but also, through your charming friend Barone Westermain-Kennedy, your doubts about the whole business. Were your skills otherwise adapted, there is no saying what might be possible.

'Anything the materialist world can't cope with it dismisses as theology. But what is the sum total of its own belief? A reduction of people – souls – to figures in a ledger. And then there comes a great void, when we are disrupted and people don't behave like that. Karl Marx was in his way on our side. He was religious, in the sense of believing in rules. Or you could at least read between his lines. What we now have – is it American, through the 'pictures'? – isn't an improvement on the old bloodfeud. Bloodfeuds imply a sort of control. But, Dr Moore, I am rushing ahead. Matters still have to be moderated after the old Emperor . . .'

Muir found, amid this atmosphere of religious competitiveness, marketeering almost, that he could not dismiss from his mind the rituals of 30 November 1916, retold by John Reede:

the black catafalque edging its way through the inner-Vienna streets, past the limousines and staff cars of the still-Imperial government, and that strange ceremony at the door of the Capuchin crypt, so arcane and at the end so touching. The Chamberlain walking forward:

'Who knocks on this door?'

'Francis Joseph of Bourbon-Habsburg, Emperor of Austria, Apostolic King of Hungary, Count of Bohemia, Duke of Lodomeria, Prince of Dalmatia, Count of the Veneto and of Lombardy . . .'

To which the waiting monk replied,

'*Ich kenne Sie nicht.*'

'I know you not.'

The Chamberlain stepped back to the catafalque, then came forward, knocked again.

'Who knocks on this door?'

'Francis Joseph of Bourbon-Habsburg, Emperor of Austria, Apostolic King of Hungary, Count of Bohemia, etc.

Again,

'*Ich kenne Sie nicht.*'

He came forward for the third time,

'*Wer klopft an diesem Tur?*'

'*Ein arme und suendige Mensch.*'

'Who knocks on this door?'

'A poor and sinful creature.'

'Enter.'

Kaiser William, in comparison, seemed English, a monstrous golf club bore; like Kipling whose brilliance in print sank under his embarrassing politics.

The flow of conversation paused. Muir noted a certain nervosity in his companion. This gave way to alertness when the noise of a car grinding up the road intruded on them. It ceased. Then there were footsteps and the thud of the outer door closing. A middle-aged, bespectacled clergyman entered, clad in a simple black soutane.

'Your Holiness.' said Pallanzi and fell on one knee, Muir followed him.

'Doctor Muir.' Pope Benedict the Fifteenth gave a weary smile.

'So kind of you to make the journey. Doctor Muir, you can depend on the discretion of my staff. So far Britain's government has unfortunately been discouraging to my feeble effort to drag humanity back from self-destruction. But it was undertaken with goodwill, and I note that some at least of your leading diplomats do at least grant me that. And indeed your fellow-engineer from Glasgow, Mr Arthur Henderson MP, seems to have similar ideas.'

Muir bowed.

'Eminence. There is only the slightest of chances. Believe me. As an engineer I know that once a machine as elaborate as the one we think we command locks into action, it is difficult if not impossible to stop. There might just be a conjunction that enables it.'

It was odd to trace the origins of this demarche back to Lloyd George's eventful private life and influence of the Sisters Reid. Yet presumably earlier Popes, not just the worldlier ones of the Renaissance, had dealt with similar constellations of eros and dust: crusader knights not far from the predators on Viking galleys; pious mistresses of autocrats, and so on.

Benedict resumed,

'Religion will continue, however awkwardly, while women and sorrow exist in the world. And there has been an excess of sorrow in recent years, caused in so many ways by that rationality that was supposed to produce prosperity. What may emerge is perhaps its obverse. A bluntening of all the emotions, so that hecatombs of death produce no exceptional reactions.

'In other words, Dr Muir, if we halt this war now, the damage will be containable, on the level of one of last century's wars. If we allow it to continue, the dead could be counted in tens of millions, and the trauma – the effects of the crash – would be greater still. I fear the kindling of *sacro egoismo* – a religion not of generosity but of varying combinations of self-love and social hate.

'We may be easy enough to mock. We pledge ourselves to the service of our people, foreswearing the pleasures of love and sexuality – in which some of my predecessors were expert.'

He gave a thin smile.

'Are we misleading ourselves? Are we so limited as never to ask that question? Or do we believe that we can sublimate our desires to serve? To provide channels of selflessness to enable people to recover from what the economic flow has brought to them?

'But I have little time. Forgive me if I don't argue but give out doctrine.' The voice was quiet, preoccupied.

'You wouldn't expect conversation, I think, but a text to reflect on: a tabernacle not a roofless cathedral of incomplete discourse. We have our clouds of witnesses in your own country, not all of them reliable or impartial or even wholly sane, but they have taught me.

'Our Church has its presence. It is a serious house on serious ground, though it always has had a sense of the extreme. You might as industrialist or technician see your present task as a war to be won. You have gone energetically towards this. Around me there are many to whom it is part of the Latter Days: to whom there is no stopping place – no relief from social and moral dissolution. The war you try to win, at huge cost to your own house of Scotland, if I judge your reversion from pruning-hooks back to spears, may soon be lost again, and on far worse terms. People we judge secular and civilised may turn on each other like cannibals.

'In some senses you may be right, believing there is no place for my Church and the values it represents, just a series of more or less harmless institutions for the relief of useless members of the Italian middle class? It may be so. Sometimes I ask myself: has the recovery of my Church since Pope Leo been at the expense of that Italian democracy that seemed so alive at the time of Mazzini and Garibaldi?

'*Porro unum necessarium.* The necessity is for some sense of the permanent. In this city we are instinct with ritual and ceremony. I walk into our churches – the smaller ones rather than Great St. Peter's: St. John Lateran, maybe, or little St. Peter in Chains – and see not perhaps belief but a space made for God by Michelangelo or Bramante. What space, Dr Muir, have you made? I don't ask this as a challenge, for I can see an honourable answer on your behalf: your ships bring food, feed people, provision and extend your huge cities. Your railways and warehouses and dams and waterworks enable them to live materially. But how does that end: in those hygienic human rubbish-dumps around our cities, where machine-cut stone records your triumphs for a few visitors as your body rots? On in mistakes as final as a train smash, which accelerate this process?

'I think you are asking yourself the same question, or you wouldn't be here. You may be able to show your opponent a way out, messy, temporary, but you are almost certainly too late – though you have at least responded to my plea and that of the Empire which was my reflex and for much of the time my opponent. You will, I fear, fail, but you may learn from the failure, so you must not give up. I wish you well and bless you. *Nisi Dominus, frustra aedificavit.*'

Benedict made the sign of the cross, and bowed to Muir, then he gave a little cough and, somewhat flustered, made for the door. The car started, but its noise was then broken in on and drowned by the rattle and clatter of a passing cavalry troop. Pallanzi took Muir's hand. 'We will do what we can.'

June 1917: Father Rothschild SJ

Then, minutes later, something untoward. The noise of another motor on the Via Roncalli, of brakes, footsteps and the door opening. There entered a short, rubicund, prematurely white-haired figure: instantly recognisable to both graduates of Cambridge as Father Roger Rothschild SJ. Pallanzi remained composed, though the flicker of an eyelid told of disapproval. Muir thought about why he had no prevision of this. Rothschild was all over him in seconds.

141

'Ah Duncan, Father Gray in Morningside told me you were expected in Rome and, having a conference of the Society to attend, I inquired in Oxford – Milner invited me to the Merton Feast – and Father D'Arcy reckoned you might be here at San Anselmo. What a marvellous coincidence!'

Muir thought of the swan, queen of the river, gliding along serenely, with its webbed feet threshing around below. Had Rothschild hired special trains, even planes, to get here?

'We are always surprised by the ignorance of the Berlin High Command and Military Cabinet. Wrong about social context, wrong to divert effort to the Middle East.'

Only when the dust of the Dardanelles cleared did the extent of your Scottish mobilisation become apparent. A whole economy put on to a war footing. What stuff! I have seen material from Abwehr reports to Berlin and from their Irish and socialist friends proving this. The Irish rising was botched, and only rescued for them by our superlatively inept British military.'

'There is, however,' the Jesuit continued, 'another, subtler resistance, hinted at by Colonel Buchan. It might go back to Disraeli: the threat of a war economy going unbalanced, of a European conservatism breaking down into ethnic nationalism and releasing atavistic militarism and racism.'

From this Muir concluded he was (quite rightly) suspected of secretly pursuing a compromise peace. For the next week Father Rothschild's diminutive figure seemed to haunt him, stepping from an office he was about to visit, waiting on the down platform at Castelgandolfo as he arrived on the train from Rome, and so on.

'Various causes have been born in this conflagration. Despite the bestiality of the fighting, on land and on sea, mere destruction is boring. It doesn't hold the attention, let alone stiffen up the sinews.'

Of course he knew Westermain. 'A Catholic scholar of the Austro-Scotch, vastly wealthy, mystically nationalist. 'Might have been worrying, Muir, on your fringes.' 'How, I wonder, does such a man fit into Clyde mobilisation and the war effort?'

'He fraternises with inventors and is caught up in the science of the first and in the second by the Lloyd George effect, not least because he owns much of South Wales.'

Muir then kept silence, but guessed that another questionmark now posed itself against him, namely his own involvement with Westermain.

July 1917: the Sued-Tirol, Dialogues

Still, words had been spoken and a day later Muir reached Verona aerodrome and *Modernismo*. Confronted with the triple-engined bombing plane, he could see the progress that had been forced through in the months since he had started work as armourer. There was a cabin for a crew of four, which was heated – albeit by the central engine's exhaust. A solid wingspan bore up three heavy engine nacelles. Nothing fragile of the experimental-aviator's time remained. This was matter-of-fact, brutal. The ground war – glimpsed later from high above – seemed ant-like, scrappy and primitive.

The Caproni roared heavily along the landing strip and then lugged itself into the air, perilously close, he thought, to the fringe of the pine-forest.

Treating for peace was bold and in some eyes treasonable – 'If successful', the boss had implied to Haldane in Downing Street, 'it is my idea. If not, it's yours.'

Footage from Pathe News glossily developed gave a clearer picture of what went on . A fortnight later Muir watched it in a newsreel theatre at Euston, saw the titles, inwardly heard the voices, tired and unhopeful, of the Habsburg official drift back to him:

'We have tried, but apart from the Holy Father, no combatants other than our Empire show any interest in negotiations. Further, our war party has been strengthened by the recent victories, and troops moving back from the Eastern Front.'

And the official from the trade union federation:

'The social-democratic parties, the trade unions, realise that they can gain more by the war continuing. They were poorly paid. In the case of woman workers often not paid at all. The war has given them status and bargaining power. They fear that a peace will consolidate the old aristocratic order.'

'The dynasty?'

'Our young Emperor Karl is enthusiastic but immature. The Slavs, north and south, are no longer at our table. Doctor Muir, your academic friends did their work well; they have encouraged the national spirit, but they have not brought peace.'

Muir emerged from his reverie as the last frames showed the two negotiators walking towards the plane and mounting into its cabin, and the plane taking off. Decades later, he could claim authorship of a new cliché.

August 1918: the Atholl Palace Hydro

Glasgow had suddenly become the City of Dreadful Knights, and Sir Duncan Muir was among them. But first there was 'post-war reconstruction'. Innocent enough, and hopeful-sounding. Neither Connie nor he actually thought so, as they prepared for the impending meeting of industrialists; Muir donning his scarce-worn RNVR Lieutenant-Commander uniform while Connie elaborated on their boss' new allies amongst the Tories:

'Dai's press-lord friends keep tabs on their associates. You can always find out the latest ideas from them. One line being discussed in the unions is a system of co-op ownership, like Cole and his Guild Socialists.'

Constance had turned up at Park Terrace that evening, without boss who was busy planning a Peace Conference. She gave Duncan a lift.

She drove well while he was barely competent – and in four hours, by Stirling and Perth they reached Pitlochry. The twin-pepperpots of the Hydro commanded the valley on the east, the gravel court before them was crowded with new saloon cars. Sir James Lithgow's was elderly and modest.

As was his speech, delivered in a hurried monotone, rhetoric not being his forte.

'The problem is that we can now make planes and machine-guns and tanks – endlessly – but there's not going to be much demand for any of them.' Remembering that his brother-in-law Adam Nimmo was no more helpful, talking colliery closures and buying, post-reparation, new mines in the Ruhrgebiet.

'And at the same time, Chairman, we will have to cope with the ex-servicemen, *dying* to get back to the jobs they used to have.'

Muir eyed the gathering. The uniforms had diminished, but also the corduroys and tweeds of his engineering territorials. Apart from Connie, not a woman in sight.

He glanced down from the tower window. A large bottlegreen Rolls-Royce was coming up from Pitlochry. He recognised it and shuddered. Minutes later there was the noise of heavy, if hesitant steps, and Sir John Kierlaw propelled himself to the table-head, to a collective indrawing of breath. Kierlaw was less aristo than Boyar. He was old when Gladstone died: pulling fortunes from his antiquated cotton mills in the Vale of Leven and investing in racehorses and actresses, boxers and football teams: Stock Conservative, from the Orange Lodges to the 'betting papers' of the Clyde. His eye was glaucous, his voice quavered, but the hand grasping an ebony cane looked supple enough to snap any foe's neck.

He loathed the left but praised as 'a practical socialist' . . . Signor Mussolini. He cawed:

'Gentlemen, let me put it bluntly. We made a pile out of the war. They tried to bring us down but we survived. We're now well-enough padded; we will shortly have a sympathetic government. 'Being well-meaning' means on all sides 'running at a loss'. Our industry has changed totally since August 1914. Everything logical makes me want to ship my cash to Zurich and equipment to Italy, and follow it. Labour is now a power in the land when it should not be. It will bid for control, and we should and must defeat it.'

Muir cited coalition promises, following on the franchise "homes fit for heroes", better public health, a new school system . . .' but was conscious that Kierlaw had the floor:

'And how do we *pay* for all this? We have no obligations to them. I don't subscribe to this democratic dopeyness. We are the result of a Darwinian selection, and will live. That is *natural law*. Those trade unionists don't represent democracy but a minor interest . . .'.

Muir: 'They have votes they can exercise, and coalition Liberals like myself will soon be under fire if we can't satisfy their reasonable demands. We campaigned for slum clearance, and having cleared the slums, we will look idiots if we don't build.'

Kierlaw: But costs are high; we have the miners on our back; we have this explicitly socialist government *leadership*. Remember what Mr Lloyd George has told organised Labour whenever he had the chance: 'Boys, I'm one of you.'

Muir's 'round table' was going down like a lead balloon. Approaching victory meant Lloyd George was now the whipping boy. More, and this was embarrassing, he communicated with him through Connie, and it was difficult to see where the sex ended and the politics began.

From his table he saw the almost physical tendency of the room to flow towards Kierlaw. And then, out of the window, there was Connie leading Buchan, in his colonel's uniform, along the terrace. Minutes later he was in the room, looking fretful, and with some relief Muir put young David Paterson into the chair . . . to paralyse Scottish industry for two decades.

'Duncan, sorry to butt in,' Buchan interjected *sotto voce*, 'but I was visiting mother and Anna at Broughton, had to go on to Inverness for a Northern Barrage presentation. Thought I'd pre-empt the cable from Beaverbrook you'll get. First the good news. Sam Raingo's leaving the government. Or rather he's dying. You're going back to London as Minister of Records. Cabinet rank.'

'If that's the good, what's the bad?'

'Henderson still hasn't surfaced over there. What's worse, Beaverbrook has got material from Germany that shows a 'mole' in your department. And, you will know this yourself, Duncan, by now: there's that personal issue.'

Helena, then, and the reckoning. He wasn't alone among the old peace party, but now seemed almost symmetrically nailed, compromised by cold new forces – and that quartet: Halley had disappeared, Helena had become his opposite number in Berlin; rumour had Bob, his stalwart at the yard, with the Bolsheviks in Moscow: from harmony and hope into chaos.

Buchan was ruefully sympathetic, glanced at the retreating flotilla of big cars, shrugged his shoulders and lit cigarettes for the three of them.

How we live now . . . Big, mechanical, unforgiving. Caught between Christopher Wren and Ollie Hardy. 'Si monumentum requiris', or 'Another fine mess you've got us into.'

5

Eastern Approaches

Of arms and men, and succession states,
in Dimitrious Makropoulos's country

'Weiaa – boom! Boom! BOOM! Weiaa-Weiaa-Weiaa – BATOUM!!!!!'

Dr Mavor's demonstration of Grand Strategy, with accompaniment (more Wilson, Keppel and Betty than *Scheherazade*) certainly rivetted his late-night audience in the Western Club, Glasgow.

'Just when you thought, boys, it was all over, a new three-letter word to cause merry hell. Forget W-A-R think O-I-L!

'What you need for your cars and buses and liners and airships and planes, phonogram records and cine-film and suspenders!

'And who's got it?'

'Not us but the mysterious Orient . . . (further sand-dance routine) – or the red Red RUSSIANS (Cossack Dance and cacophony)!

Applause! Applause!

And, he added obliquely, to Muir as they drank cocktails at the bar. 'That's where I'm off to.'

October 1918: Westermain Redux

'Check.' gloomed Westermain. 'In practically every direction:

amounting to total paralysis. Would it have been different if we'd got into play before the Americans?'

'This was the problem. Our support was potentially huge: think of the power of the Catholic Church, and the recognition of the Pope. But there was no dynamism behind it. D'you remember *Hadrian IV*, that strange book by the madman Corvo? It was daft but no dafter than the Hollywood movies. Sooner or later someone will get that religious-social gospel out of the Vatican's cold store and find that there are takers.'

Muir, summoned telegraphically, hastened through an eupeptic West End to Kintyre House in Mayfair, entering as it turned out on its last decade. He found Westermain in the smoking-room, slumped in his chair. Red hair curiously grey-streaked, red-faced after his ride, his gold-wire specs folded in fat, for he'd put on weight. He had the superficial air of a Hogarth squire.

Only superficially? There was a new forlornness: marriage on economic impulse (the sheer size of his palace literally fell on him) to Sarah Raingo, Sam's daughter-in-law and after her husband's death in the flu epidemic his heiress. Not wise: it was almost instantly plunged in distrust and alienation. She delayed, dissimulated and ultimately refused – understandably but with determination – to start a family or go north to Westermain.

'That wind would kill me. You wouldn't want to put me and baby in danger?'

Already bored with her, Westermain was still capitalised on a level which would make a Balkan finance-minister drool.

'Look, Duncan, you've been wrecked; we've been wrecked. Lloyd George has settled with the leaders of the succession states of the dismantled Austia-Hungry empire; Masaryk, Paderewski, Karolyi, etc., backed up by Bob Seton-Watson, Bryce, and so on. Not a chance of saving Old Vienna, let alone Old Rome. Making matters worse, the German general staff – the most right-wing thing on the planet –

unleashes the Bolsheviks in Russia, liquored-up on ideology-spiked-with-electricity and bound Godknowswhere. Your good self *nearly* manages to fashion the old order, a diplomatic weapon, but Vatican 'mediation' is ignored – even when it might have saved Vienna and the Irish Union . . .'

'But the League, Quentin. You should get that at least out of Paris? Your lecture-tours?'

Westermain was patently uninterested in the career that Lord Bryce – founding father of the League of Nations – had chosen for him. Oratory had its limits.

'I wanted great diplomatic strokes – *demarches, bouleversements.* I wanted the old order to survive by re-engaging itself, because I thought it could still do so. But what do we have? Lloyd George, Orlando, Clemenceau, Wilson. I know the first and last. Lloyd George was dynamic, now burnt-out. Met Wilson once. He cycled to Peveril, our Cumbrian place. Gave him afternoon tea. Grandfather was a minister in Carlisle I think. Mother was from the family of Robert Wodrow: *Troubles of the Covenanting Kirk* or some such. You wanted to be impressed, but here was a boring, touchy, semi-educated man . . .'

Old age hath yet his honour and his toil;
Death closes all: but something ere the end,
Some work of noble note, may yet be done,
Not unbecoming men that strove with Gods.

Oh no . . . Muir thought, glancing at the books and the Black Sea maps, Kinglake's *Eothen*, Mackinder's *Geographical Pivot*, piled on the low table, a holstered revolver as paperweight. We were in for a last romance; just when the rational investment of the Kintyre millions was needed and would prove a safe bet. The dramas of the war – that universal jangling of nerves – had conjured Westermain into a sort of phantasmagoric breakout – out of Kipling's *Man who would be King*, Buchan's friend Sandy Arbuthnot, strange new magi . . . Gurdjieff, Ouspensky.

Also, more mechanically, it was as if the switches in that other Kipling poem hadn't locked but were sending Westermain's train at full speed down the wrong line. Human impulse or error could sort itself out. This couldn't.

November 1918, Athens: Major Mackenzie takes stock

'How big, exactly, is this place? Two hundred thousand?' asked Lieutenant Saunders Lewis, 'Bigger than Cardiff I suppose. If we can imagine Cardiff minus coal . . .'

'But plus lots of new-wrapped Germanic classicism.' Major Compton Mackenzie, in his pale tunic and Sam Browne belt, stood in the oriel window, looking from the administrative centre down on Plaka and, in the distance, the Parthenon cut against a thunderous evening sky. An electric tram whined out from behind a plane tree, encountered a flock of loutish, yellow-grey sheep, stopped. A red-haired man in a uniform and cloak descended.

'There's Kennedy.'

Mackenzie filled and lit his pipe and puffed it into a glow. An Edinburgh blend of Virginia and Latakia perfumed the high-ceilinged room.

'And in the near future, there will be a lot of merchants from the old Ottoman Christian communities looking hungrily at Cardiff's business. These boys have been trading since they invented it. Mention a word and they give you a price.'

He put on his glasses and read a cable.

'At last. Salonika. Our buried army breaks from the tomb: that'll kybosh Bulgarian communications. They'll surrender in days. Habsburgs next. Saunders?'

'May I stick with trade for the moment? This morning a man came to see me about a ship called the *Petrolia*. Greenock-built oil tanker, lying ownerless at Piraeus – her boss went down with her sister-ship – but still Glasgow registered. Oil gives about double the energy per ton of the coal we get on the boats from Cardiff. She isn't going to interest our man, but there's also a 500-ton passenger-cargo boat, the *Propontis* . . .

'Who's your man?'

'Dimitrios Makropoulos of Smyrna, at the Athena Hotel.'

Mackenzie took the card, glanced at it, put it in his wallet.

'Saunders: always distrust hotel post-restantes: the plusher, the more suspicious. I've met Makropoulos. None the worse of a hanging. Too charming, oily as his tanker. Something about his manner told me he'd dishonoured women and killed men. We may hear more about him – I fear.

'These new exiles – and there will be exiles, exiles and massacres – have trade in their blood, relatives to feed. They look for partners. Our war-millionaires want to bank their winnings, present their daughters at court, head for the golf-course and – if they're really deranged – the huntin' field.'

'Matter in hand is now in the downstairs waiting room. Quentin Kennedy Westermain . . .

Drop Kennedy, dear boy: now stands for a Boston precinct captain with ambitions and a restless cock.'

'Westermain's a bit wrung out after the FO's deal with Masaryk and the Czechs, not to speak of Arthur Balfour encouraging Rothschild and the Zionists. All happening very fast, and without any of our old Levanter hands at the tiller. Disraeli was a long time back, but he knew his way about this powder-keg. Downing Street doesn't. Westermain still thinks he's in with a throw.'

'Discourage him Saunders. We've enough problems.'

'But we want to get the White Russians back fighting, so why not the notion of some sort of pluralist settlement?'

'Attach Quentin to the Great Game? Get him to ally with Dunsterville and his forces protecting the oil fields at Baku?'

'We could do worse. At least with his dough, Quentin won't cost.'

'This time I'll pull rank. Wish me luck.'

Minutes later, Mackenzie was back, thoughtful and initially unforthcoming.

'Will he see Makropoulos about that boat? Did you try to persuade Westermain of our scheme?'

'That matter, Saunders, is now out of our hands. Westermain has letters. C. in C. Eastern Med reckons he's probably suicidal but could help delay the Bolsheviki: keep 'em out of Poland and Finland. I told him about the oil in the Caucasus. But no, he has promises to keep . . . to some bunch of Anatolian tribesmen, Christian, he's convinced himself. In happier days his uncle had sailed there. He has a bit of one of their tabernacles in that mad castle of his. He says he knows what the risks are.'

'God help him.'

'Precisely.'

January 1919: Berlin, '*Trotz Alledem*!'

Helena woke up. She had slept fully-clad for days it seemed. Hoar frost had invaded the inside of the windows in the borrowed flat. Outside, snow and ice, precipitated from grey sky, crusted the roofs. Only wisps of steam from ventilators showed where life was going on. A fine day to die, she thought: a morbidity that stemmed from hunger and illness as much as political peril. She could do it quite easily, drinking enough schnapps to get to sleep, wriggling herself into a ball like her cat – long departed, but probably still alive – in a remote corner of a park, or somewhere in the acres of empty coal sidings. But *Requiem aeternum* had to give way to the duty of destruction.

Tod ist der Meister in Deutschland. It wasn't just the war, ending in humiliation but also the vengeance of the Right against the socialists who might be inspired by the Russians; the personal as well as public exhaustion; the Spanish influenza galloping through the place like something out of Duerer; the suicide – was it suicide? – on 9th November 1918 of Alfred Ballin, the Atlantic liner tycoon who might have been a midwife to the new Republic, but was dragged under by his war record, a peace broker, his fleet of cruise ships ferrying the dispossessed of Europe across the Atlantic a victim of his own country's U-Boat torpedos.

The disappearance – capture? probable death? – of her lover Kuno Liebeskind in this fundamentally aimless revolt. To endure seemed purposeless. Better to take risks to stop others dying.

Two days before, in one of the long circuits she made to avoid the right-wing Freikorps, she had unexpectedly found Theodor Fontane's grave in the French Cemetary. Modest, black marble, buergerlich. She remembered lines, found long ago with Bob Cormack on a Fifeshire grave. They came back to her in what she knew would be her last hours:

> *Fear no more the heat of the sun*
> *Nor the furious winter's rages;*
> *Thou thy worldly task hath done,*
> *Home art gone, and ta'en thy wages.*

Bob had read them out: the dead Italian woman in cold, winter-clamped Fife.

'Her man went out to fight alongside Garibaldi. She came back with him, but she didn't last long.'

'D'you know that's Shakespeare?'

'No. From where?'

'*Cymbeline.*'

'Clever girl.'

The city, even in imperial days, even during the war, had never been like this. The barrack-like blocks – *mietkaserne* – seemingly had closed their faces to the street. Life went on behind the curtains, but didn't proclaim itself. You glanced at strangers and passers-by for the danger-signs of 'the Right': a duelling-scar on a cheek, the way a woman wore a scarf. There was little fuel around, so anything on wheels was automatically suspect. Armoured cars, favourites with the ex-army *Freikorps*, were noisy and slow, giving plenty of warning.

Rigged out like a *Putzfrau* – boots, shawl, dark overcoat, shopping-bag, Brandenburg patois as rank as anything in a Fontane novel – she managed to reach the party HQ in Kreuzberg unbothered by anyone official. The stair was empty, the flats prudently evacuated, though there was no evidence yet of enemy, like bullet-holes or scorch-marks. The office was cold, the central heating dead: the point wasn't to restart it but to destroy as much of the material as the enemy might need to identify the members. The more she wrecked – of what she had built up, painstakingly, over her double-life of the last year the more she would have achieved.

Even in the ghastly circumstances, the paradox amused her.

'Two party members, one of whom is an MP, have less in common than two MPs, one of whom is a *Sozi*.'

A dynamic had been built up. When she thought about it, rather like what her Clydeside friends had managed, insofar as a record could be consulted in these Dutch or Swiss safe-houses. Labour had bought-in to government. 'Lions led by Donkeys': but the donkeys had won the vote, from dopey George Windsor downwards. Here in Berlin, partly thanks to her and Groener, the Lions had taken over, pretty efficiently. 'Blood and ironworkers.' But generals and trade union bosses had seen-off Petrograd and Moscow. As dear Bob would have put it,

'They weren't havin' that.'

The files. How to get rid of them? There was no fireplace. If she started a fire, it would spread and eight or nine families might lose everything. But there was a secret place under the floorboards where Kuno habitually left letters he didn't want others to see, and there was an unaddressed envelope:

My darling,

I got here last night, but they were on my tail, and I have time only to leave this. You will find paraffin in the right-hand cupboard in the cellar. There's a clothes-boiler in the yard: outside and to the right. Pile the stuff from drawers one to four loosely in the stove, soak it and it should go up in about five minutes. I wish I could say there was somewhere safe to go to, but there isn't. They'll probably have found me by the time you get this.

Liebchen Ade. Trotz Alledem!

K.

'For a' that!' Shakespeare and now Burns.

She did as instructed, though the process seemed endless, as typescript and holograph notes singed, creased, and at last turned to ash. Then she found a big file of Central Committee minutes Kuno had overlooked. It was heavy and somewhat damp, and took nearly an hour to dismember, crumple, dry and burn. But burn it did, and thus saved lives. 'In my end is my beginning.'

She heard the noise. The heavy engine of an armoured car and what she dreaded, the squeal of brakes. Boots stamped up the close. Nothing for it but to face death, like Fontane's old Dubslav von Stechlin, last of the lairds, in that cold dawn twenty years before, out in the province. Engelke, his last servant, had brought him snowdrops. The thought made her composed and appraising, though nothing grew in that icy yard.

The door burst open and the last thing she saw before the machine-gun bullets hit her was the furious face of Oberst von Stumm,

'You stupid pricks!'

He yelled at his standard-issue, crop-headed Kameradschaft.

'You fucking animals! If we'd had that woman for half an hour we could have got the whole bloody lot out of her.'

'*Judenin?*'

'*Nein. Judenhure!*'

He kicked the body, and Helena's face swung into view.

'*Sie lachelt sogar!*'

January 1919: Trabzon: Roth's Opinions

'I smile at all this.' Herr Roth, Austrian Novelist, occupied a corner table in the nearly empty winter-garden of the Hotel Imperial and McCann's. This evening he entertained Dr Mavor who had hitched a seaplane ride from Batoum on the Black Sea. There was little business and the relative grandeur came cheap. He took an early morning walk along the *Platanenallee* that girt the bay, slept, had a cutlet and salad to eat at seven, then wrote and smoked steadily, igniting each fag from the glow of the one previous. He got through a bottle of whisky a night. This evening he made it two.

'Residual links with Britain? Here? Maybe.' Mavor wanted stuff on Westermain-Kennedy, and his time in Trabzon. He could take Roth's leisurely scene-shifting: 'Clerks on high stools like those in London, but wearing fezzes; drifting in by tram from suburb villas *a la francais*, which pretty quickly pitch down to hen-runs and scrub gardens. Town centres with marble banks and post offices, dog-eared adverts for RAGTIME! or JAZZ! on the iron conveniences.'

'Beyond these an authority subsisted that stretched as far as the telegraph wires. From time to time, but lasting for hours, a monotonous line of music emanating from an inner court seemed to express a quiet, despairing expectancy, but not of joy or fulfilment . . .

'What chance them against the new order? Young "social scientists" who plan to lose so many out of a population. The necessary dead. With us it would have happened by accident. Act of God, Act of War. This lot set out to carry their industrialisation. They decide. A third are simply going to die. Can't be sentimental! But the old man Francis Josef wouldn't have done this.'

'At the end of it all?'

'I got to know "Kenadin", as they call him. He came here disciplined and sober, which I'm not. His ship no good, same went for his allies: ready to piss off when the geld ran out. Stayed here for weeks, waiting. Would walk out along the sea-front, stare out, looking for a ship. Your guns, Kennedy. They never came. Poured himself a drink. Talked to Madame's girls; didn't do anything more, though he patronised a different one each week. He was generous, they said. They protected him, the girls: gave him baths, showed their tits. He didn't want more. "And they never let on what I'd told them." He helped them with their tax and the police. Then he went.'

'Despite everything, he managed to acquire a tramp-steamer. It had come up here looking for a return cargo of grain. But the war had scared off the harvest people. Stuff rotted in the fields. So the ship was going cheap. *Helvetia* she was. Sound enough and quite modern, Glasgow-built, for your friend Sir Muir – who passes as some sort of a red? Even the diesel engine was an advantage, for there was damn all coal left.

'Trouble was that there was only rubbish about in the streets. Youngsters who hadn't shipped anywhere, fatherless because of the war. Just lazed about and lived off their sisters, faces always in the dark. Narrow, watch-your-back eyes. The stub of fag ground out in the dirt, substituting for the eyeball of a rival.

'Kennedy? Holy Joe? He got cables that said there'd be a White troop-train at your Batoum; enough fuel on it to get them half-way across Georgia. They get there and the train's gone; not another expected in weeks. They got a shunting engine and some of the marooned wagons, lopped down trees in the park, got some carriages for their crazy gang. Then off into the mountains, hoping that the last Bolshevik train hadn't ripped up the track. As far as I know they're still on the go. Rumours spread round them like a rock thrown in a dark pool.'

25 January 1919: Burns Night in Moscow

Peter Petrov, ambulant revolutionary, chased out of Glasgow, realised that in the Kremlin you survived because of who you knew. To hell with conviction: the leader had his Committee of Public Safety and the others were expendable: appointed to remote units, simply imprisoned or killed. He made himself useful by using the big heating furnace at the Technical High School to good purpose and for a time he enjoyed Lenin's favour, though never trust. If he could get the latter, even for a short while, he *might* safely 'leak out of the landscape'.

In between, in late January 1919, he organised a Burns Supper. Chicherin and Litvinov helped. They knew Scots journalists in London. Someone raided a White HQ and stole their whisky, mostly rotgut but with a crate of half-decent blends. And then there was this Music Hall turn that Bruce Lockhart, the British *attaché*, had unearthed, who was *sui generis* . . . though what a memory act was doing in Moscow was a mystery.

'An' ah hiv tae say, a mystery t'me, too. Colonel Buchan had gaun too far this time. Whit wis ah daen' in mid-winter in this freezin' place, wi' nae snug pubs or obligin' girls? Till ah wised up. Ah wisna' there tae spy oan the Rushians but oan the Tommies. An' ah wisnae hae'n that. An' jist at the moment o' realisation, whae dae ah merk but the man interpretin' for Commandant Trotsky wis an auld freen frae Glesca Trades Cooncil, name o' Wullie Earsman, the same that had been for years in Australia stirring up no' very much. He turns oot tae be like *that* wi' Peter Petrov, whae also had his Glesca' moments, so I got a message to Colonel B that I'd dae a planned skedaddle doon the line tae Moscow, spier aboot for a wee while, an' get back to him.'

'So there I am wi' Petrov an' Mrs P – no' in her first youth but a fine lookin' woman, owrecomin' communications problems through a taste for black furs an' showin' her legs a lot.'

So it's 'Tam o'Shanter' an 'Holy Wullie' in return for an audience wi' the big an' bad, an a few mornins' wi' the beautiful. Ah could ha' dune worse.'

Anyway there we are in her man's bed wi him awa' fechtin' in Poland an us workin' at a bottle o' Crimean champagne in between the usual, an' she asks div ah ken Burns? An in view of the situation ah comes back wi' 'Nine inch'll please a lady.'

Which she doesna' completely grasp (no knowin' oor measures) at first, then laughs her heid aff, coorse jaud. But why's she keen?

'He didna' write that gash maist o' the time.'

Ah telt her as best as ah' could aboot his sangs o' luve an' freedom. She says somethin' like "Vladimir Ilyich loove Burns" an I get the idea that ah could work this wan, helping her man Peter at the same time.'

So – Why no' a Burns Supper in the Kremlin?

'Double-plus-good idea,' says she.

'Eh?'

'English too complicated, say Irish comrade O'Brien: too many words. So we simplify. No more "really good" or "marvellous". Instead have a scale: very good equals plus-good. Marvellous good equals double-plus-good. Simple, is it not? So Burns according to Lenin equals double-plus-good.'

'Whit wis I?'

'Double-plus-plus-good, sweetie.'

'Ye dinnae argue wi that. Maist like, it winnae catch oan, but ah didnae want an argiment neither, so ah held ma wheesht.'

'So then it happens – gang forrard a fortnicht – in wan o' the biggest ha's in the place. They're a' therr, frae auld Prince Kropotkin tae Trotsky, an the vodka's going sooth like Irn-Bru.

'Chicherin does the Immortal Memory wi' great respec'. Hadna' he lived near twenty year in Hampstead? Fred Engels couldnae hae dune better, an' he was faimly, or near enough. Then there's Lenin an' Krupskaya in the toast to the lasses an' the reply, very coquettish-like an dead worrying – though there I have the feelin' that that show's noo rinnin' oot o' road.

An suddenly . . . Joe Stalin gets oan his feet, an in English tae:

Breathes there the man with soul so dead,
That never to himself hath said,
"This is my own, my native land!"
. . .

Near tae tears, but Chicherin mumbles something like 'That's no Burns, it's Walter Scott.' Lenin digs him in the ribs,

'Fuckin' shut up, or he'll have you on a slow train to Sakhalin – if ye're lucky!'

'Then there's the dancing, wi' Leon Davidovitch Trotsky as caller an' a gang o' Yankee Wobblies tryin' tae smuggle in squerr-dances – lots o' clappin' an throwin yir legs ower yir shouthers an that. He let it go wi' the flow – ah'm no sure whether the tunes were Scots nor Rushian nor Mongolian but he fair belted them oot, givin' the drums laldie.'

An that's the queer thing. Him the great thinker somehow respondit tae the music yon scratch band threw at him, stridin oot like an Emperor wi' the grand slow tunes, an knockin' sparks oot o' the flerr wi' the dervish bits, till ye couldna help stampin' an clappin. An the gimlet eyes behin' the glasses, first hard an concentrated, then gettin' caught up in the music. Then a' mindit the tune, an it wasna' Russian at a' but oot o' Hungary, whit Bob Cormack had played in yon wee toun in Renfrew seven year back. An a' thocht o' Helena and whit we'd heard o' her end.

Stalin wisnae lookin' happy, so efter a coupla slow numbers, Natasha rubbin' her wee tum wherr' it mattered, we cleared oot. An spent the hale nicht in bed, no sleepin' much, in which the workers' revolution split fae heid tae fit, Stalin an' Trotsky at it like cats. Next mornin', fore Joe can grab him, Trotsky's in his command train wi' steam up at the Kazan Station, heidit sooth. There's a revolt on the go by the Caspian near the Georgian oilfields led by a gey strange Cossack holy man ca'd Pretender Kenadin or some such.

Petrov's away back to Poland and gifts Bob tae an armoured train. Whae answers ma ring at the flat door, wearin' a black fur coat wi' no a stitch on under it. Am ah no the lucky comrade!

Winter 1919: With the Armoured Train

Picture the huge train, *tovarichi*: fourteen carriages, two locomotives, crew, workshops. But, first, the 'dumb wagons' – in case of mines, the heavy naval guns in their turrets, machine-guns behind them. Then the engine and generators. Saloon carriages for the commissars, the troops, their staff, petrol tankers for the armoured cars, stacks of skis and sledges. The press and printing wagon. The cinematograph. The pigeon-loft (thanks to an English comrade!) Comrade Commandant Leon Davidovich's office. The sleeping cars, the stable cars, the provender cars. There are bands here, and teachers, instructors and judges. This is a government on the rails.

The line had been severed by the war during the summer months. Theirs was the first train for some time.

And now you would never know
There was once a road through the woods . . .

The Kipling lines came back to Bob Cormack as the snowplough beneath him sheared through young growth, which made their track scarcely different from the six or seven other overgrown ways that beckoned at clearings. Never before had he felt actually indebted to a railway which, however unkempt, knew where it was going.

Then the train crept on to a landscape of unbroken white. Sky undifferentiated from what might be plain or lake. As if to emphasise the fact, the ice and frozen snow cracked and snapped before them, its shards lifting up and then being crushed by the advance, however slow, of the locomotive. Commissar-Bob, on the railed platform above the snowplough, peered forward. The telegraph wires were not, as normal, a guide, for they had gone off to the right, where he guessed there was a village, or more likely the house of some magnate.

'Consider it lucky that we don't follow them, friend, probably into some prince's stables. In the old days, money drew the maps.' said the young Bolshevik by his side.

The two stood outlined against the white, only their eyes visible, and their breath. Behind them the great flared spark-arrester chimney, and the complicated, waddling mechanics of a heavy goods engine.

Yevgrav was an engineer-lieutenant. Young, Bob guessed, perhaps no more than twenty, if that.

'Franco-Belge, Liege, nineteen-o-eight.' He said, 'Relax, Commissar-Bob, there are spare parts, in the fifth wagon, and there is the plane.

'The plane? You have a plane?'

'In the fourteenth wagon. It's in pieces, but Comrade Lagulin said they were all there. We found it in the White Barracks at Kiev. We have petrol in wagon fifteen.'

Somewhere called Vortilovna was ahead, as long as the railway still led there. A gamble, said Yevgrav. Indeed, two hundred yards ahead, a foot of ice gave way to a surge of brown water as a river – temporary? permanent? – not noted on their small-scale map, crossed the track. Bob got the driver to cut steam and sent an infantryman plodding back to the second engine as they rumbled to a halt. They couldn't risk the water reaching the lead firebox; so banked the fires and were pushed by the rear engine. This edging-forward took two hours.

Vortilovna had an engine-shed, and a couple of Frenchified

buildings, one a boarded-up hotel, the other a burnt-out bank. Smoke rose more reassuringly from other low wooden houses. Locals nerved themselves to come to the station, out of commercial acumen – babushkas with baskets of eggs, piroshki, smoked meat, sausages – curiosity, residual sense of public duty (the Hetman and his confederates) or boredom. Vortilova had had its history, quite recently.

'When did the Whites leave?'

'Ten days ago. In a hurry.'

Commissar Yevgrav sent out details to round up locals to get firewood. There was the usual scene with a puffed-up Hetman but, once Yevgrav threatened to summon a firing squad, the usual surrender. Within two hours four bogie-trucks, groaning with wood, had been marshalled between the lead engine and Lev Davidovich's saloon. A score of 'volunteers' were housed in a passenger car. Conscripts? Hostages? Bob did not ask.

After another four days a pale ridge of mountains showed above new ridges of trees, still very distant.

'She was German. She went back, and she disappeared at the end of the war.'

'What happened?'

Bob shook his head.

'I heard a month ago she'd probably been killed. When they put your people down.'

'The Spartacists?'

Sonya was dressed in dark trousers tucked into heavy boots and a shapeless blue tunic. Only there was, at the throat, something that might have been a hint of a paisley-pattern lining. She folded the lapel back. It showed a whorly red-and gold pattern.

'We like this. We don't boast about clothes or fashion like the old order, but in the lining of our jackets we have something of our own, a bit of an old dress or a scarf, or a memory of a baby . . .'

Sonya ran the dining car. Usually the province of incompetent, frequently drunken men and dragon-women, she was as the Russians would say *krassivy* – valuable, clever. She imposed order on the kitchen car, to produce substantial meat stews by dint of fierce bargaining at the stops, and well-aimed shots from the soldiers which hit inquisitive or simply unfortunate animals. She conscripted others to accompany her to the markets in the towns and by a combination of threat and charm stocked up her larder with fresh vegetables and jar after jar of the preserved fungi, salads and fruit so beloved of the Russians as *zakutski*, flat-bread, little savoury pies, smoked fish. German beer replaced vodka. She was supposed to have something going with Commander Trotsky, which helped.

Bob reckoned the real power was Trotsky's lieutenant who called himself O'Brien but whom he had known – at a distance, in Glasgow Trades Council – as Lucas Kelly. The depute Commissar, once flamboyant, was now pared down to the systematic apparatchik.

'O'Brien. My mother's name. They like you to adopt these "struggle-names", like Lenin or Trotsky, or the "Man of Steel . . .

. . . once you have co-ordination, you acquire a new logic, which your opponents are unlikely to break. They cannot appeal to the people. We can – or at least once we have the productive system running properly. But we must live with it, see it from the inside, develop it. If you give that up everything will fall apart, and they'll kill us all. As happened to your friend in Germany.'

Everything quite logical. He tapped his teeth with a silver propelling pencil while making his responses.

'We have to gain industry, and indeed rapidly. Potentially electrify: all these great rivers. We have initiative, enthusiasm. We know the dynamos of capitalism; but we will not make the same mistakes.'

Bob was les convinced, 'They said that in the last century, too, and you know where that got Ireland. A million dead in the 1840s, when a quarter-million were building the railways in Britain.'

'The revolution enables us to cut into this tangle with a surgeon's knife. No interest to shareholders, or pensions to bankers and their kin. Instead, let them pay a ransom to those who, as a mass, are their victims.'

'And casualties? Can you plan for these?'

O'Brien's dialogues with Bob as chief engineer were carried out over the chessboard. Neither was much good and Bob reckoned that of the two he was perhaps the better. But in this game it was best to learn how to lose convincingly.

On the board, he observed a threatening combination of queen backing up a dual rook-bishop gambit. His king was fenced in behind pawns and checked.

He won the first game, but guessed O'Brien had allowed him to do so, entrancing him into his dark wood.

'Miss Sonya – Comrade Sonya, will be the prize.' This might be a joke, he reckoned O'Brien as keener on power than on desire.

'Forget it, O'Brien, you've already lost that.'

'So be it.'

Cormack was not trustful. Which was putting it mildly, as he told Sonya, when she came by his cabin after dinner.

'He's aff his heid.'

'He's a sad man, but he worries me. Can I come in and worry you, too?'

Thereafter she would come to his brake van every night, after she had fed the crew: with something hot and a litre of beer. She used it to polish her English.

'The Soviets will win and I hope they will reform. On the other hand rich Whites will clear out and they'll want cooks. If I organise, I'll win either way.'

She had come from near-extinguished gentry near Taganrog on the Black Sea, her mother was partly Baltic German.

'Nothing ever happened there. A big decrepit house half-a-day's ride from the station, an overgrown orchard. An old bore of a professor and poor uncle Jack trying to keep the accounts, periodically hitting the juice. Once he tried shooting the Prof but missed. Good on him.

'Aunt Frances made things worse. Drained the place like a leech for her theatre productions, then had to sell up. I got a scholarship to the Smolny Institute in Petrograd, to study cooking. Best choice I ever made.'

There had been a fiance who vanished on the Finnish front. The rules of the Russian small gentry were strict, and she was still a virgin when the war broke out. Then there had been a lover among Lenin's staff: neither exciting nor trustworthy, it seemed – 'You get kept in a cupboard. But it could have been worse. I got this train-set as a present.' And she smiled. To her cookery Bob added his fiddle-playing, and their evenings became a sort of free house for the younger folk, of food and music and – if they weren't too tired – dancing. She had a face somewhat heavy at the throat, and irregular teeth, but she smiled with her eyes, she charmed and Bob found that the longer you talked to her the more animated she got, and this so expressed her adaptive, complex character, as someone once said of that other girlfriend: not pretty, but beautiful.

'Our place was a mess, but the characters! Some of them seemed to look beyond our plains and woods into the infinite, and not just because they were daft or drunk. We had books and pictures; we put on theatricals.'

'You had the advantage – aa' these infinite steppes. Try dae'in plays in a single-end.'

Bob found, as the train ran slowly south, he got used to Sonya present, fretful over Sonya absent: first for practical language and catering reasons, later missing her, to talk to and talk back. He noticed also that her utilitarian costume – partly due to their reaching the warmer south – had begun to feminise itself with the products of her Singer.

Life on the train was a sort of a village community, with Comrade-General Leon Davidovitch as a sort of landlord, intermittently absentee as he tried to establish where the elusive Kenadin was. O'Brien filled in, imperceptibly expanded his empire. Bob as the engineer became a sort of hetman to Sonya as quartermistress. There were seventy on the train and he made sure he knew them all, from firemen to Commissars . . . yet was always diplomatic enough to present the Russians, Comrade O'Brien now included, as leaders.

Thus developed the legend of *How the South was Won* as the Vertov Studio would present it a decade later, after Bob and Yevgrav pieced together the Bristol Bombardier from Wagon 14 on the platform of renamed Kropotkin, within sight of the white rampart of the Caucasus.

11 April 1919: The Bridge at Vezenar

'Various arguments on both sides,' said O' Brien, cogent for once and alarmingly so. He had used the restored telegraph to contact Moscow, but seemed to have inputs of his own from the Cossack *freischarlers* who crossed their path. He sat impassive, enigmatic, questionably sane, on his saloon car's veranda as his interpreters interrogated.

'Kenadin the Holy Man is about 300 miles off in the mountains. He holds – or at any rate has a train on – the Baku-Batoum railway. Who he is we don't know. Another True Dmitri? Enough of these in the Russian past. Or a prophet? This time there seems to be a Mussulman side to it. Add to that the Persian oil gushers. *The forces that'll bring us Armageddon are subtly massing.*'

From this Bob concluded

'There are various toxins in this from those German campaigns early in the war, the stuff in Hannay's Greenmantle business. The Germans were much taken by old MacKinder's 'heartland' propaganda. So we sent some modern planes out to Russia. They seem to have disappeared.'

'They haven't.' said Yevgrav.

Bob found this when he inspected Carriage Fourteen. A two-seater Bristol Bombardier fighter-bomber sat there, in a crate. He and Yevgrav, who had been an engineer-pilot on Sikorski's giant 'Ilya Mourometz' bombers, took it out, displayed it before O'Brien, who saw that it was good.

They fiddled around with it when a loco breakdown stalled them at Vorodin. A raid on an isolated mansion whose millionaire owner had cleared off yielded enough kerosene drums for two or three days' use. The Bombardier had been ingeniously built on a 'completely-knocked-down' principle, and Bob found his time served at Beardmore's on light-oil engines and aboard the 'Blackness Castle' had helped. By five in the afternoon a test-flight was possible.

'Can we get out to that line by plane and see where Kenadin is and where we might stop him?' O'Brien was moved enough to transfer the plane from tactics to strategy. On the map, the line wriggled along the sea-coast and crossed the mountains in loops and spirals.

Tomorrow would tell whether they could.

'Kenadin's train's at Kashgar. Problems with their locomotives, might be delayed two days. He's captured some of our medium guns so he could do damage to any towns on the way. He has promises of help from local magnates if he can get his train through. If we can get a hundred miles farther south, we should be able to survey Kashgar-Baku and try to stop him on that stretch. Wreck the bridges. Far-fetched but not impossible. D'you think you could do it?'

O'Brien turned to Bob.

'Mebbe possible, but only just.'

'He is the last hope of the Whites. The last vessel of that putrefying atavism of particularism and tribalism we are sweeping away.'

Bob wanted to say, 'Ye aince worked for him, Luke Kelly. More, ye fought against owremighty empire in Dublin. Noo ye soun' like a Free Kirk missionary.'

It was a cold spring, but this at least meant that the land hadn't thawed into mud. The plane could take off from any of the provincial roads near the rail track. It was just a question of Yevgrav's competence as a pilot. The pair reactivated the fragile construction, taxied it cautiously up and down the dirt road.

'You will take care . . . ?' said Sonya, and the fact that she was that worried about him helped Bob's morale.

The flight was brief, serving only to try the engine out and show what railways and trains looked like at such and such a distance: about seventy miles to the Baku railway. Maybe a further hundred to Kenadin's train.

Prospecting likely targets, bridges in particular: if they could find one which was timber, they were in with a chance. The line's double-Fairlie engines had been built in Glasgow at the N B Loco's Hyde Park works and Bob remembered their odd 'push-me pull-you' appearance. Their big flared smokestacks also suggested wood-burners so with any luck the bridges would also be wood.

The Bristol Bombardier had on the morning of 11 April enough juice for two trips: one reconnaissance and one attack. With any luck, O'Brien's train would have moved fifty miles closer. Bob packed extra kerosene and a couple of 12-lb bombs, just in case.

The Bridge at Vezenar: the Movie

It is in the nature of this narrative to leap back and forth in time, and in 1929 Bob and Sonya Cormack had an evening free to go up to Glasgow for a film show organised by the ILP at the Cosmo Cinema, famed for putting on things like Fritz Lang's *Siegfried w*ith full orchestra. A series of Russian films was on, mainly Eisenstein, but first a short called 'How the South was Won' by a pupil of Vertov no-one had heard of.

The small orchestra was going its dinger at its Russian repertoire and on screen a posse of Whites in Black Hats were leering and table-thumping: cross-cuts to paunches, vestments, houris dancing on tables, etc. Titles were sparing: but after a bit of topographical, folkloric foreplay, children helping with the harvest, crones gossiping, the story got going:

Under the fanatic Kenadin the reactionaries mobilise

Lots of soldiers with bedrolls and wickedly long bayonets. Then the Internationale and from left and way back a column of smoke, materialising into an armoured train.

Bob squeezed Sonya's hand.

'Looks familiar. But . . .'

'I wonder.'

A grouping of stern young men round a table in a saloon car. Panning from face to determined face

Their opponents: a tiny band but brave, conscious and convinced . . .

Mixes of mountains, telegraph wires, Lenin, lorries running, grinning, waving troops off to the Kazan station. The quartet managing to get the right national anthem at last. Then the whole armoured train caboodle seen from above, rotated under a spinning biplane.

The south would be taken by the new power of the air!

'God! It *is* us!' though they were of course all actors, the Academy and Meyerhold's best: blond-mop Vassily with his grin, thin saturnine Gavrilo: best buddies. Vassily family man with cute kids, Gavrilo with teacher-lover and lots of tendresse.

A magic-box sequence in which, out of a crate, a biplane constructs itself, cuts from antique Cossacks, drumming hooves, to clean-shaven pilot, montage of propellors blurring into red – then red-tinted flags flown from aeroplane and train:

The revolutionary heroes take off into an unknown country

(Bob remembered the morning as clear, cold. At first the land below them looked almost undifferentiated in terms of pale grey-green, then the sun picked out white-ochreous snowfields, little red-and-white villages.)

Their plane spots the counter-revolutionary train aiming for the Batoum Soviet

(They reached where the western railway ought to be, and a plume of smoke showed the Kenadin train fifty miles further east than expected, within striking distance of Baku. No chance then of a proper return bombing trip. They dropped to under 100 feet and the rails showed up rusty and overgrown, but still usable.)

The revolutionaries overtake the White train and reach the little station of Vezenar.

Open-mouthed, the actors seek out the Vezenar station staff. The real place: with its ravine and the plateau on which a plane might land.

Pray God the bridge is wood!

The film bridge was a toy, though realistic enough. The real thing had been metal, replaced after sabotage by heavily-creosoted trestles, but not, like *their* one, roofed, American-style, against the snows.

The piano rattles away to represent the bumpy landing and taxi to a standstill.

Vezenar station is deserted – like the Marie Celeste. Breakfast laid out, grate still warm.

A lot of mooching about with revolvers cocked, Western-style. Our heroes find the single van in a siding:

'Enough wood here to use as kindling. Forty minutes in hand.'

They listen for the noise of the enemy train.

(Bob remembered from Hyde Park the soft double-exhaust – woof-woof! woof-woof! – of the Fairlie, though there was no sign of smoke or steam above the eastern woods.

'We fire the bridge. They have enough time to stop.' While Yevgrav prepared the waggon, he fixed a combination of detonators and dynamite inside the roofed section. The van, as it rolled down the slope, would trigger them.)

In the deserted engine-shed they find cotton waste, oil, detonators – and a pinch-bar

The two heave frenziedly on the long-handled wedge, used as a jack to get the wheels in motion. Near-microscopic shots of rusty wheels moving almost imperceptibly. Foreheads beaded with aweat. They stow the combustibles with

Half a dozen sticks of dynamite – to 'make sure'.

The van starts to shift. Cut from some peasant ploughing-fest, happy oxen, to Kenadin off his head on the train veranda, stabbing the air with a steak-knife.

The enemy approaches.

The White Train's exhaust is now real and audible – with the quartet bass going woof-WOOF! woof-WOOF! Grey smoke-plume navigates the mountainside terrace, about two miles off.

The van's wheels start to move. It trundles slowly down the grade to where the embankment to the viaduct starts, began, Vassily and Gavrilo running alongside with their hands on the brake.

(Bob dropped the lever and the van squealed to a halt. He fired three cartridges from his Verey pistol into it. A flash of magnesium, a gush of choking orange smoke, unpromising flames. Was the wood or the cotton-waste damp?

They had maybe thirty minutes in hand.

'Bring the plane over! He shouted to Yevgrav, and they bumped the thing across the yard (ten minutes) then tied it to the tracks (five minutes). Then as he worked the pinch-bar, Yevgrav banged the aircraft engine full on.

The van started to move. Two minutes of propeller-backdraught directed at it turned it roaring red with flame. In a further minute it headed slowly over the trestle towards the roofed bridge.

The Kenadin armoured train clanked and screeched out of its cutting, rounded a tight curve. It stopped. Smoke was by now pouring from the bridge. Yevgrav brought the Bombardier onto the dirt road and idled the engine.

'Bob!'

Bob was signalling to the enemy, waving his shirt.

'Dinnae go in, ye stupid buggers!'

The first three trucks and the engine detached themselves. Riflemen opened up.

'Bob! The big gun!'

There was a loud bang as a shell burst between him and the bridge, thank God obscuring him as a target. He ran like hell to the plane.

'They're no gaun' in?' Bob shouted to Yevgraf. 'Goad, they're daft!'

Yevgrav opened the engine up and the plane roared along the dirt road and into the air.)

The heroes look at one another in despair. Then resolution
There is only one way out!

Montage of Gavrilo's girl, bare-breasted, stretching her arms out to him, Valeri's little blond poppets playing with him on the lawn.

Cut to the White train and satanic Kenadin, long hair, dark glasses, big bad feral teeth, snarling commands to a crew of ghouls.

Gavrilo and Valeri hang on to the truck. It gathers speed. The White Train, blasting smoke into the air, roars towards it. Cut after cut to – and from – Kenadin: locomotive: gun recoiling: resolute heroes: smoke: snipers: heroes: hands grip brake: heroes: hands on red flag:

RED COVERS SCREEN; SHEET OF WHITE: THUNDERCLAP

envelopes timbers, van, gun-carriage, locomotive, carriages – then tiny sticks which might have been human or debris tumble and twindle into the ravine. Kenadin, ringed with flame, burns into a skull. The carnage framed in the biplane's wings, a propeller which loses speed and stops.

(As they looped back, circling to gain height, a small explosion caused the bridge roof to collapse. The trestles fell over seemingly in slow motion, carrying the waggons and ultimately the locomotive. A cluster of survivors peered into a chasm of smoke and swirling flame, and up at the angel of death.

In the Cosmo Cinema Bob turned to Sonya,

'Wasnae like that at aa'. I tried tae stop yon train. Aa they young folk deid, an Hyde Park's best work ...')

After the battle on the bridge, the Kenadin conspiracy shrivelled. The film could end with peasants scything a sunlit field.

It was a case of hunting then down. O'Brien was triumphant – and that triumph would serve him well where party lines had to be trod, for forty years. It would only be a matter of time. Sonya and Bob had to entertain him, and administratively that went well. The problem was that alcohol and familiarity pushed the barriers too far, though its conjuncture brought grace to their own situation.

O'Brien pushed the last half-empty bottle of Crimean red to his silent Chinese aide and returned to his corpses:

'Clovis had someone once in his life. A soldier who died in South Africa. Not killed: a minor wound that went septic because of disorganisation. Clovis was kind, and rather timid. He said "When I think about you I think about warmth, security, what old Whitman or Addington Symonds wanted from their lads. It's all canted over by our screwed-up emotions. Buggery and violence in the boarding schools; the violence compressed into our lives. Kept at bay by drink."

'We visited these odd women in Manchester: Eva Gore-Booth and her friend Hester: "This is our office. And we sell stuff here for the garden and keep the books of the co-op. You could call it a relationshop. I've nothing against babies, nor has Evie. We look after lots of kids at the settlement. But I don't want a life dominated by them. I don't fancy looking after a man and getting a child because he's careless. There are good men, Luke. You're OK; Helena fancies you something rotten, but you're her inaccessible pinnacle. That seem Freudian enough? But you're not Evie. I love her."

"Stuff." snorts Evie, and then smiles.

'That was the odd thing.' O'Brien was reflective, sentimental, frightening. 'These two women radiated love. Whereas men –

Englishmen in particular – share pain. Not periods and childbirth and the menopause, but messy, incalculable pain: having a mine-gallery fall on you, being swept off a trawler, losing a hand in a machine. I wanted to be Evie-Hester but the world of Clovis and his aunts was a concentration of this savagery.

'If I couldn't have it I wanted to inflict and feel pain. Real pain. That's what Clovis wanted, and *then* I had no such desires. It was more than masochism; it reflected his social position, his grim, contested view of . . . everything . . . So I understand people like Cortiss, who wrecked his life and our chances. Part of me wants to destroy people like that, and enjoy it. So it wants an ideal big enough to validate that violence. Pay it back in kind. As if I wanted a civil war in Britain. Which – reading *News from Nowhere* – millions dead for Morris's arty-crafty world – I did.

'So I hate holy fools like Quentin Kennedy and selfish studs like Duncan Muir. Westermain's crusade consorted him with the dead, with the detritus of old empires, his corpse-bride: he doesn't see the vicious priests who wasted lives for their crazy power structure. Muir's worse. Likes his wine, fucks his women, who love him for it – 'the wee rascal', they call him – and organises destruction on an unholy scale. Unctuous swine, regressing like Kipling to his gears and screws.

'Tonight, I have signed my rescripts and through them I kill God – and God knows how many – then that Chinaman will come into my room and punish me: inflict all the pain he can, by whatever means: to the point of maiming, but not beyond it, for a set time. I will gag myself so that I cannot stop it. Sooner or later enemies will take me and not observe any time-limit. But I will know what to expect.

'These are the latter days, Comrade Cormack. Old inhibitions don't apply.'

April 1919: Love in Caucasia

That, they both remembered for the rest of their lives, was the night they, in Sonya's term 'got together'. After Vezenar Bob 'wasna himsel' – but out of mutual desire, Sonya's good food, the alcohol, the warm room and the flickering orange glow of the wood-stove, and sheer horror at O'Brien – 'Oh God the man's dreadful. This is Sexton Blake stuff!' – they collapsed without speech into one another's arms. It was one of those occasions, beloved in the movies, where the act of love ought to make everything whole again but Sonya had to work hard with someone who ought logically to have been traumatised. She was grateful to badhat lovers, their sentimental pornography, even to a generally unbearable mistress of the craft like la Ranevskaya, observed in action as far as several bedroom doors. Bob sensibly allowed the wine and the woman to take over – 'Don't worry, just cuddle, get used to me. Like this.'

An amorous grapple brought him to her breasts, which were well-shaped, with nipples like raspberries. After all, in one day he'd learned flying and fighting. Why not . . .

'Love means kisses in special places.'

This worked, and she drew him to her thighs and the tangle of her love-hair.

'It's what Ovid says, the boy gets his pleasure from the joy of his girl. All that matters is yoni and lingam. And yours is working very very well.'

'I practise a lot on my own.'

'And you haven't gone blind, my love. So now begin, open the doors and begin ... Do it now!'

In the pleasures of the sexual act inhibitions about 'lovely', 'nice', etc. disappear. The results needn't be recorded, but a bit of Bible-reading never comes amiss:

A bundle of myrrh *is* my well-beloved unto me; he shall lie all night betwixt my breasts. Behold thou *art* fair, my love; behold thou *art* fair;

yea pleasant; thou *hast* dove's eyes; also our bed is green. The beams of our house *are* cedar, *and* our rafters of fir.

'But O'Brien! *OGottoGott!*'

'He's Romford.'

'Eh?'

'Five stations on frae Barking.'

'There's probably genius there, but I don't want to be around when he fires up.'

'We've got to get out of this place, if it's the last thing we ever do?'

'Well put.'

They made love twice more, then Sonya went to sleep with his leg trapped under her bum, and he got a horrible cramp prising it free. Hirpling around, he found a blanket to put over her bare shoulders, and squinted through the curtains. Dawn, cloudless and at this point greenish in hue, was coming up over the Black Sea.

Bob dressed and stepped down from the saloon, hoping that the Chinaman would overdo things before O'Brien got into his stride. The train stood on a siding which ran on into a decaying dockyard. There was a rhythmic sucking, clicking noise from the air-brake on the locomotive which he found oddly satisfying. Yevgrav gave him a mock salute from the footplate. 'A fine day, Comrade Bob, after a fine night!'

Elaborate concrete buildings were filled with inexplicable apparatus, in various stages of discolouration and decay. Ponds of viscous greeny-brown slime, the occasional dead animal. The rails ran out along a mole whose seaward side consisted of a jumble of concrete blocks and bits of demolition rubble. All was silent but the rails were powdered by pale yellow rust.

Three-quarters the way along the mole was a battery of cranes, and a black-funnelled tramp which had, over the previous week, discharged five thousand tons of steam coal in clouds of dust and grit. The SS 'Dyffryn', Captain Goronwy Edwards Evans Llanfrothen, Cardiganshire, had before 1914 usually sailed from here with grain, and Captain Evans was considering a proposition by the local military governor for a cargo of grain to Beirut, minus a huge personal backhander, and the very immediate problem that his Chief Engineer had disappeared, trying to prove that he was as incompetent blind-drunk as he was when sober.

He had not expected a well-qualified, well-spoken Scotchman to turn up. Least of all on this forlorn quayside. Nor had he expected him to cable Sir Daniel Stevenson personally in Glasgow *and* get a grain contract from Constanza to Swansea *and* a return steam-coal cargo to Piraeus. No up-front bonuses involved, only the businesslike proposition that he exercise his civil power and marry Chief Engineer Cormack to his betrothed before they sailed.

May 1919: near Batoum

That Bolshevik air attack was the last straw, and Westermain had no hope for himself. The Reds had won hands down, but instead of despair this made the waiting endurable. The point was not to break. He approached one of the Bolsheviks whom he believed spoke some English, and passed along the files to a bespectacled Scots-Australian in a saloon car who claimed to be on Trotsky's staff. The commander of the armoured train was a Lucas O' Brien the Bridoonstown man? – who did not appear.

'You are?'

'Quentin Kennedy, once Lord Westermain. It doesn't matter now. You are?'

'Willie Earsman.'

Earsman was East Scottish, then Australian, so it didn't matter anyway. Westermain was an arcane enough figure, even in Glasgow. He handed over the letters.

'Two people. Duncan Muir you may know.'

'You're no gonnae get oot. We've orders to hang ye a' before we leave themorra. We're that incompetent that ye'll take a long time to die. So take thae pills and this bottle tae wash them doon. It should do the trick . . .

'That's the simple wey, but there's always them as winnae take it. There are other things ye can dae with the booze an' pills, an' this bunch o' animals arenae the smartest in the zoo. Mind, I've never seen ye.'

Earsman accepted the little silver cross, and forgot about it. Long years later, he was in a trade union delegation to Muir, as Depute Shipbuilding Controller in 1942, and asked him if he knew the initials on it. Muir did. It cleared up a little more of the story, but not all.

As it was, the last moments, two days later, were panic-ridden. The day was clear and cold, the wind whipped the bright blue water into crests which crackled like ice. In mid-morning the dust of White Russian armoured cars could be seen against the dark forests to the west. Puffs of smoke were followed by jagged fountains as their shells tried to get range. The armoured train got steam up, O'Brien signed a sheaf of rescripts.

A detachment swung ropes over the burnt-out canopy of the station, and the half-dozen condemned men were ordered onto beer-crates and noosed. Then they kicked away the crates. That was that.

Or was it? A couple of years later Muir was at a dinner with Buchan, who told a tale he had recently picked up from a Royal Scots squaddie who had been captured by the Turks at Kut and surprisingly both survived (hardly anyone else among the rankers did) and escaped. He made his way north-east to a White-held zone on the Caspian seaboard and found himself in a narrow street jammed with a huge Orthodox

religious procession – 'A' that gowd an' croons' an' canopies an' singin'
. . . An' there was this great big man wi' glasses an' a lang red beard
swingin' wan o' they centaurs, y'know they incest-things, back an'
forth, a' the time singin', broad as the Clyde,

"If it does ye nae guid, it'll dae ye nae hairm!'"

6

Resurrections

Round table to Covenant,
'Among new men, strange faces, other minds.'

Dumbarton 1919: HMS Wombat

'Like other portions of the Empire, Scotland has suffered from
the weariness produced by stupendous effort and impatience
which has found vent in industrial disputes and in an eager
adoption by some of the youth, of new social ideals, in which the
influence of Russian Bolshevik experiments and propaganda
has been conspicuous.'

'Weel said, Principal Rait', said Andrew Amos, reading the *Glasgow Herald* while playing crew to Muir, as the *Dalriada* scooted out from Dunoon to spectate on the trials of HMS *Wombat*.

'Mind you, yon disnae look like any sortae ship tae me . . . A drookit lorry mair like.'

Muir, on the other hand, felt sympathetic to, even sorry for, the *Wombat*, his latest and probably last project. Particularly since there was now no chance of building the thing in series, with the end of war production. David Paterson, competent enough as Ballantyne Muir's lawyer, had thought and thought and suggested various routes to survival. The ones that worked led away from the Clyde.

The habit of things going wrong, particularly with oil and explosives around, had influenced Muir. There had been enough disasters, and they hadn't managed to cover all of them up. On the technical side, there was a need for a sort of marine handyman, which could sort out the mess that war and war production left behind it. *Wombat* was a robust seagoing barge, lacking shape or grace, with a pram bow, wide platform for carrying things on – buoys, lorries, packing-cases – a big diesel generator, a hydraulic crane controlled by electric servers, and a swivelling electric motor at the stern. You could carry and service donkey motors and divers on it (interestingly, you could never call it 'she') or passengers – in or out of a bus – at a pinch.

Amos who had taken over from Bob Cormack at Ballantyne Muir had applied himself to test it on the river, and reckoned it a winner – 'at ony ither time than this.' The artist John Duncan Fergusson, current beau of Connie – '*Ci-devant maitresse*: You could call me the Josephine *de nos jours*.' – had dazzle-painted it in a jazz of blacks and browns, greens and whites so that whatever graces its 400 tons might have had disappeared altogether – which was the idea – when seen at sea.

'Things fall apart, as Yeats says, and maybe that's a good thing. A text maybe for our time?'

Over a whisky on the *Dalriada* J D F suggested a 'Wombat' class:

'Unappealing but necessary parts of creation: HMS *Dingo*, HMS *Skunk*, HMS *Ferret*, HMS *Stoat* . . .'

'Remember HMS *Monkey*?' Duncan asked.

'Come again?'

'Don't remember the poor old *Monkey*? . . .

'A tug. Built 1821. The navy's first steamer. All the Admirals hated it, headed by the First Lord, a Dundas, God help us. It would never ever be called HMS *Monkey*.'

London 1921: Allah Akhbarrie!

Colonel Sandy Lindsay, Lloyd George's new special adviser, rushed into the Whitehall office, took possession of his predecessor Muir, and bundled him into a cab. Ten minutes later they were in a narrow Chelsea Street.

'Didn't Carlyle live hereabouts?'

'Another Scottish man-of-letters awaits us.'

Not his old boss Lloyd George then. A small droopy-moustached person came to the door.

'*Wheesht.*' he said.

A minute later Churchill in a homburg hat propelled himself out of the sitting room and into the hall, into an ulster and scarf held out by a waiting servant, out of the door and into what had been their cab. A ill-tempered cloud of cigar-smoke hung in the air, drifting away to reveal various familiars.

'Sir James Barrie . . .' stumbled Muir. 'Jimmie, meet Dr Muir.' added the more soignée Lindsay, then 'Lord Haldane and Colonel Buchan you know, Mr Scott from Manchester, perhaps not.'

Barrie hurried into the sitting-room, conferred with someone and hurried back, joined seconds later by a burly young man in unwonted civvies. The latter grinned at Muir.

'Well, sir, we meet again, and in more comfortable conditions than yon damned Welsh distillery.'

Lindsay took over :

'Commandant Michael Collins, to be sure. Not these days numbered among the Lost Boys. Bunter, get Mr Collins a whiskey. Wait, you're not Bunter. Who are you?'

The dark figure that had shimmered into the lobby looked down on him with a benign understanding that seemed almost super-natural.

'An Irish whiskey or a Scotch malt whisky, sir? They are said by connoisseurs to be equally acceptable.'

'I'll take a chance on the second.' Collins replied.

'You will not be disappointed . . . With water?'

'No soda. Out of the side.'

'Admirable. Will that serve for the other gentlemen?'

With just a touch of resolution the apparition made a slight bow and withdrew.

'Who was that? Someone from MI6?'

'Sir James's new valet. Name like Jeffs.'

Who promptly reappeared with a generous tray of tumblers and a jug of water.

'A pity the Munitions Minister couldn't stay.' offered Barrie.

'Mhmph.' replied Collins, adopting a peculiarly Scottish intonation, 'Churchill at least knows when to clear off. I'd have called him outside in a couple more minutes. When an elite starts panicking it gets really worrying. I used to hate being patronised by the English. But now, when they're scared, I get terrified. Anyway, *Slainte*!'

And the whisky-glasses clinked as Jeffs, or whatever his name was, looked on protectively.

'What you see with Churchill,' continued Collins, 'Is what you get. In fact I suppose we're not all that different: the children of adrenalin.' He gave a happy smile, which faded as his theme turned to Lloyd George.

'But there's a man born not a hundred miles from Dublin, in a place passed by hundreds of thousands of Irish every year. Has he ever crossed Anglesey to Holyhead and boarded the Dublin boat? Until last year, never.'

'But he doesn't count for all the Welsh, thank God. Here's a toast to a spirit of this house. I don't mean Peter Pan but his uncle – to Crompton Llewellyn Davies, once Lloyd George's agent, more recently our man in Dublin Castle!'

So that was it, Muir thought: not such a *feste burg* after all. Here he was, winding up the Ministry of Records, who had only months ago signed off cheques for munitions millions. And today's victor was an Irish postal clerk famed and feared in his home-made uniform, to whom capturing a Lewis-gun was a famous victory . . . and who got his intelligence from a Dublin Castle mandarin who was technically a traitor.

Just as the only popular English commander was Heroic Colonel Lawrence, a Scots-Irishman who swanned about in Arab gear making trouble for the Foreign Office. Get any group riled about being ruled – and that had become the *leitmotif* of the war – you couldn't stop them, during it or after it. From what Connie, Lysistrata-like, told him, this conviction had sapped the Coalition Cabinet, before she quit that non-marital bed.

'People say I'm past it.' said Barrie, 'Death will be an awfully big adventure and all that. But for those thousands of lost boys it came early. *There with the rest are the lads that will never grow old.*'

'Agreed, Sir James.'

Collins savoured his whisky, meditatively.

'We've a few hundred dead at most – tiny, compared with the Western Front alone, or even with the Boer War: death by incompetence. But these were people who counted, who had ideas, and the killing hasn't stopped. What I signed at Downing Street today could be my death-warrant. Dr Doyle of Bridoonstown here didn't believe anything of our stuff, really – did you, Larry? But you're getting your crack at electrification on the Shannon, and that's good Irish policy. What Dean Swift said: "Burn everything English except their coal!" The human race has been to madder places than anywhere Gulliver visited, in the last eight years.'

21 April 1923: George Square, Glasgow

'I was proceeding on my late evening patrol along the north part of George Square when at 11.43 pm I noticed two elderly Gentlemen behaving in a suspicious fashion in front of the statue of James Oswald MP, viz, thrawin' stanes at it.'

Constable Murdoch was impressive but maybe a little slow on the uptake. Bailie Bruce sighed.

'So you apprehended them?'

'They stand before ye noo.'

'Had they drink taken?'

'Aye, a fair bevvy. I'm sorry, your honour, indeed they had.'

'And have you identified them?'

'This wan says he is Peter Handy, maister o' the coastal steamer SS *Vital Spark*.'

'He's no that!'

'I beg your honour's pardon.'

'Ah've been a bailie in this court for twenty year, an' ah've had that nyaff Para Handy afore me for eighteen oot o' them. Whit wi' drinkin roon' the clock an' fraud in pretendin' that bucket o' rust o' his is seaworthy.'

'That wis the name he gied. When he wasna' shoutin' treason at his freen.'

'Treason?'

'May I quote? "Come on, thraw a stane in the auld man's hat. That wey ye become a citizen. Better still, thraw a wallet-fule o' notes. If he sits fur Glesca, he'll need it. We wan the war for them in the sooth, an noo we're – eh . . . ah'll pit it as 'bothered' – a' they frigates an' freighters an' sandbags, an' shells an' planes, but whae in the name o' . . . (we'll leave that oot, tae . . .) wants thae things noo?"'

'No' exactly treason, Constable. More a matter of common opinion. We've thoosands o' lads doon the road. An whit aboot the other panel?'

'Couldnae unnerstand a wurd. Captain Handy ca'd him Sunny Joe.'

Bailie Bruce turned to the dapper little man in a clipped beard, and nodded.

'Niam grotskesi zlin tatrienieva steamer. Soki soprotski tovirov, nyea Skoky Polacki met. Joszep Korzowieni.'

'Captain Korzowieni means I offered him a job as a deckhand on my boat. He has served in the British Merchant Marine and deems that an honour . . . , your honour.'

There was then a minor disturbance in the public gallery and the forthright voice of Sir Duncan Muir echoed from it.

'Bailie Bruce, may I be heard?'

The Bailie fell silent for nearly a minute, juggling his love of protocol with due deference to 'a Power on the Clyde'.

'You are being goosed, Bailie, by two distinguished gentlemen who might wish to avenge some uncomfortable hours as guests of the City of Glasgow . . .'

'Eh?'

'You have before you the editor of the *Glasgow Evening News* Dr Neil Munro, and Dr Joseph Conrad, a nominee for the Nobel Prize for Literature. Gentlemen, on behalf of the City, may I tender our apologies to you.'

While muttering under his breath, about what on earth had possessed them to get up to this lark.

'Waaait a minutt!' suddenly bellowed Constable Murdoch, 'Whae's wurd gaes in this Court? Yours or his or yon ither's?'

'Or mine?'

A robust pink woman's face, incredulity mixed with mirth, beamed from behind Muir.

'I am Jessie Munro. I keep and feed these two gentlemen, and a right ticket they look. Can I propose, your honour, that we adjourn *sinny die* an' all go round for a temperate lunch at Miss Cranston's in Ingram Street. They can worry aboot the Spook School wallpaper.'

'And what Munro says, my dear Conrad, is only too true.' reflected Muir as they navigated the cobbles.

'We are in a bad way, who were four years back the rulers of the seven seas. Lithgow has just made me an offer for my yard which, honestly, I can't refuse.

Down to the deid gang all estaitis:
Princes, Prelatis and Potestatis
Now dansand merrie, now like to dee,
Timor mortis conturbat me.

'Whit's that mean?' asked the Bailie.

'One o' my American friends puts it thus, Bailie Bruce: "The fear o' death sure shakes ye up", but 'shakes' wisna the word he used.'

July 1934: Watson Wilson and the last fight

Well, Sir Duncan an' me, we baith endit up as loyal comrades, but mebbe no sae loyal ... Ramsay Mac hadnae muckle tae dae wi' the Clyde, red or no, forbye it was oor boys, Jimmie Maxton an' freens, whae electit him. There was something sad aboot him. He'd lost Mrs Mac, as we ca'd her, oot o' sheer overwork – a' they committees an poor folk to keep goin', they could die aff like flies. An' aince on his own, he was fushionless. So turned oot a rerr catch for the grand life in London, a' they Marquesses, Dukes an' a' that. Kissed the magic Duchess an turned intae a puddock.

Though, fair play, he tried to get a decent deal for the puir German folk hurt by reparations and *la revanche* as that auld deil Clemenceau ca'd it. That wis when their inflation went through the roof and twenty million marks couldnae buy ye a poke o' sweeties. An' he didnae ca' Mr Gandhi a naked fakir – or worse – like Mr Churchill, efter the Dundee folk threw him out cause he couldnae' thole Prohibition. He tried tae do his best for India, did the puir soul, but his thoughts were wanderin' in an' oot o' his auld heid.

An' that's more or less whaur ye find me noo. No' in India but in 1934, efter the Germans took leave o' their senses an' let yon Hitler in. Between oorsels, the time syne 1928 hasnae been too guid to yours truly. No jist the slump but the talkies. It only needed yon Al Jolson tae say 'You ain't heard nothing yet!' an' the folk were oot o' the stalls like whippets efter a tod. An ye ken whit the Music Ha's mean tae me – no jist a show, mair a way o' life.

Then whae should turn up at ma hotel in Oxford but Colonel Buchan, noo a Tory MP tho' scarce a contentit one. Are ye free for a pair o' hours, sez he, an can we go for a daunder roon in his caur? The Disarmament talks had just fell tae bits in Geneva, an' the Colonel reckoned that Hitler wad want tae re-arm fast as he could, havin' got intae pooer thanks to thae Junker billies. Noo he has this idea that some o' his auld enemies are still up tae somethin – wrote a bit aboot it in *A Prince of the Captivity*, where his hero's a bit like puir Lord Westermain – an' gets kilt by sortae Nazis. There's this engine, for racin' planes, that could be used for fast fighters, an' he reckons the Jerries want tae get their hauns oan it.

Noo, the Colonel says some o' them know about oor dealins in the Great War. Puir Helena Mann wis some sortae double agent, closer to us than tae them, an' closest o' aa' tae the revolution: maybe why thae kilt her. Machine-gunned her an' threw her in a canal. Anyhow, if we pit the word aboot that ye're fed up, and up for daen' a bit o' memory magic, mebbe they'll bite. The money'll be guid, he says, an' I nods ma' heid, no utterly oot o' idealism cos' my auld flame Mrs Wark, Gemmill as was, wis back on the Ha's an I thought we might manage a wee guest tour tae, say, Monte Carlo when the rich dastards are there. She can shimmy roon the punters in her fishnets, askin for daft questions, an I'll dae ma bit, an something extra at night.

April 1935: To the London Palladium

Buchan cabled MacGillveray from Ottawa and they and Mavor toured out from London and met Wilson in a pub in the Chilterns. They were aware that all wasn't entirely well with Mr Memory: not in performance terms, but in ease, or the lack of it. A young woman had been murdered in London, Peter John Hannay had gone missing. Wilson was outwardly calm, but these things – and unwelcome company – didn't make for complacency.

'There's wis this political gatherin' at Merkland Ha' doon in the Borders. An' there's the owner, the grand auld Duke of Dumfries, a sortae political dinosaur, huge body, tiny brain. Skitter-skittering roon and aboot him wis a crowd o' wee advertisin' men who had got the contract to sell Chateau Ribbentrop tae us. That an' a few o' Mosley's Blackshirt gorillas whae looked after security, an' there we were sat in bluidy Balmoral wi' the rain seepin doon for a fortnicht, goin' oot daily tae blast anything that moved on the moors, an' naethin' happening, so ah'm wondering whit ah'm dae'n rinnin'alang wi' thaim.

'So, play it dumb. Dae my memory act, dinnae mak' it look as if I kent German. Then I cottoned on tae wan o' them, a lad caa'd Frankie Foss on the *Mail*. He'd done his time in Germany, an' got fair taken wi' the Nazis. Ah kept close tae him, picked up the gossip, an' let myself be pumped on yon Supermarine seaplane. I knew I'd have to wait till they verified the information. Then they'd go for the real stuff, an' I could let your lads ken aboot it.

'But the waiting, waitin' for maist o' a week, fair got tae ye. Ye had to thole a' this stuff aboot blacks an' broons and Jews, an' tae keep yersel' beltit up was fell difficult. An there was a German baron, a blond beast ca'd von Stumm, straight oot o' a catalogue, who wad hae been terrifying but tended to get that bit over-informative when he'd drink taken. Ah steyed close tae him, mebbe too close.'

Watson lit another cigarette and looked around him, and Muir became aware for the first time of the grounds for his unease.

'Something came up in the talk. No name that I kent – a Frau Goesler (couldnae hear a forename): Czech, mebbe Jewish – noo bidin' in London an' runnin' a burroo for the exiled German Social Democrats. They seemed in the past to have known her owerweel, an' boy did they hate her!

'Wan evenin' in this tomb some strangers came. Mosleyites: a mix of rugger-buggers, cockney imperialists – an' a strange blonde whae wis a general's daughter, beautiful in a cauld wey. Ah soon realised why she was there: me. Ah kent her faither in the war. A man for new ways was Major-General Max Pandy – Pansy-Pandy the coorse brutes' ca'd him, but he was clever: knew whit the new weapons could dae, thocht up strategies tae suit. Whit did he believe? Goad alane knew, but at that moment he wis well in wi' Mosley.

'Anyhow a warm bed wi' Diana an' her fifty-seeven varieties wis better than soakin masel' in the butts. If you could thole her coorse talk. Her faither fair danced roon' the tank as an idol. She didnae get any mair humane.

"Bitch divorced Clifford, a friend of Tom Mosley's. Married a gamekeeper who turned out a Red and left his wife for her."

Diana said this sprawled oot on my bed in the altogether, getting' me goin. Nipples o' iron and eyes cauld as a gull's.

'Ah did ma stuff an' it worked maist o' the time. But she went oan an' oan aboot this Goesler wumman. They were planning something against her. It wis murder but before an' after it wid be something worse. They would plant cash an' jewellery on her so that it would look as if she was tryin' to get abroad, to the USA with money ta'en frae the comrades. An' they'd got a man ca'd Drummond lined up to capture her – an' then torture an' kill her – a sadistic animal. This overjoyed them. They didn'a jist want her deid but in a way that would be an example tae ithers.

'An' then a name: "Con by name, con by nature." And I twigged. Connie. Connie Chatterley. Sir Duncan's sister-in-law, or oot o' law. No, she wasna' ane o' my conquests. I fancied her but she had settled doon wi' her George Parkin, that wis the gamekeeper, in Australia, an' after he died o' cancer, wi' the wee German Dr Goesler. She had her past but she moved on, as ah hadnae done. Wouldna' have allowed hersel' anythin' that coorse. So last week, before comin back to you, I got the word tae an auld contact o' yours in Canada, yon Adam Halley we spirited awey in 'fifteen. Von Stumm vanished afore he an' his lads could reach her.

'So you know what happened to . . . ?'

'Pit it this wey. Adam Halley, noo' cried Andrew Henderson, spiered oot in nineteen' seventeen mair than he was supposed tae. An' that wis embarrassing aince the GIs were heidit for the front. So he lighted on me wi' this stuff, an' I helped him vanish again. It wis last month an me fixin' the wey oot for the Goeslers that's caused the problem. Ah've lost ane o' ma nine lives.

'So that's it. Aff to the London Palladium for an evenin' o' gallantry an' intrigue. Gie the false stuff tae Chateau Ribbentrop's boys, an' with luck they'll be in Berlin afore they find oot. Then oor side can round up the Black Stone gang over here. Or so we hope.'

April 1935: Dissecting Mr Memory

'The bullet struck him in the lung. It wasn't in itself fatal. Had he been kept quiet he might have pulled through.' In the cold room Dr Mavor replaced the sheet. 'But it was a case o' "gonnae no do that", as we say up there.'

'It was compulsive, in his character?'

'What he was programmed to do, you mean?'

Mavor thought it might be something more. Somewhere in the brain of 'Mr Memory' there was a sort of central technological membrane, observable back in 1915. In 1935 he was trying to work it out, in a world gone out of control, with mad ideologies of race-destruction, possible atom bombs. He had his suburban life and wife, plus the Music Halls, his obliging chorus girls. MacGillivray and Buchan had got him out to stop the Nazis getting hold of the details of the Spitfire engines. But Muir thought he would have, in that strange almost mystic way he remembered from 1915, gone beyond. He rang MacGillivray.

'Mac, do you remember how Wattie used to 'place' his technologies within a strategy. It was something he did to help memory.'

'Yessss . . . But it wasn't his real forte: something he was good, or very articulate, at.'

'May I persevere? I think what he gasped out begged one central question. If the engines worked in that way, their power could only keep a plane aloft for about half an hour. OK?'

'They would certainly require to be precisely targeted at their enemy.'

'Does such a technology exist? You know how Wattie would scan his way through the papers, but return only to the direct questions.'

'Leave it with me.'

A few hours later the phone rang.

'Mac here. We have some of Wattie's notes referring to a research project which involves bouncing radio frequencies off incoming planes, reading off speeds, altitude and so on. Doesn't help bombers, so boss-man Lord Trenchard and the RAF establishment weren't interested.'

'They'd bloody better be. Do we know who to contact?'

'Someone called Watson-Watt, strange to say . . .'

Autumn 1939: British Columbia, diminuendo ...

Around Governor-General Lord Tweedmuir's train, parked in a siding, there reigned the silence of the Fraser River valley, apart from the muffled thrum of the generator, and the strains of cello and fiddle coming from the state saloon.

'Wisnae easy, rescoring yon without puir Helena's viola.'

Bob Cormack had remarkably swept down on a freight from the Kennikat works, where he had been rebuilding a dragline excavator. Adam Halley holed up for years in a cabin high above the siding, taught rural economics by correspondence course.

'Music's lost on me.' Said John Buchan, a slender, almost wraith-like presence, 'My limit was "Three Blind Mice".'

'Think what you might have done with Wagner, John.'

'I tried, but Wagner's not my style and I'm tone-deaf. Susan and I did a sort of feelgood Valhalla 'The Island of Sheep' in 1919 but it didn't work and nobody read it thank God. The Ring's as bloody as the

Border ballads, but with none of the jokes or that cosmic bleakness that puts you in your place:

> *Ower his white banes, when they are bare,*
> *The wunds sall blaw for evermair.*

Hence our present troubles.'

Why was this going on, thousands of miles from the Clyde? Reasons of State, planning aircrew training, on and off aircraft carriers, and here was Sir Duncan Muir to explain them. Back in Edinburgh he had been installed in the Scottish Office's vast new headquarters (well out of bomber range), got Regional Commissioner Tom Johnston to realise what - years before – Westermain's strange young man Robertson had been on about, and leant on Hore-Belisha and Liddell Hart at the War Office. Two decades after the Japanese Admiralty had debriefed Robertson's associate Forbes-Sempill (they kept him as a consultant way past Pearl Harbour) it dawned on boffins in small back rooms what had actually come to pass, under the Germanically-abbreviating *Blitzkrieg*...

> *The man that hath no music in himself*
> *Nor is not moved with concord of sweet sounds,*
> *Is fit for treasons, stratagems and spoils;*
> *The motions of his spirit are dull as night,*
> *And his affections dark as Erebus.*
> *Let no such man be trusted*...

Shakespeare sounded good, but the disrupter of the Venetian aristos was a Jew, Shylock. If 'Harmony' was to be enforced against him? The Rainbow Bridge of the Clyde wasn't magic but made out of treaties and cartels and conferences. Total war had broken through these. Muir had seen this in front of his nose. The next would be worse.

In the beating of Berlin, the outturn had been due to a contest between averagely unimaginative men given an accession of force no-one could control: 'gangsters and shiny-bottomed bureaucrats' George Orwell (a Dalriadan of sorts, on Jura . . .) called the Nazis. Both sides had them, and magicians whose acts wore thin.

They were tired out but they knew the ropes, could still do the stuff, one last time. Would *Dalriada* lie quiet, the Clyde yards and foundries silent? . . . Yes but not quite yet.

Melrose, 12 February 2015.